Drift

Brian Castro was born in Hong Kong in 1950 of Portuguese, English/Chinese parents and came to Australia in 1961. He began publishing short stories from 1970 and is the author of the novels *Birds of Passage* (1983), joint winner of the Australian/Vogel literary award, *Pomeroy* (1990), *Double-Wolf* (1991), winner of the Age Fiction Prize and two Victorian Premier's Awards, and *After China,* which won the Vance Palmer Prize for Fiction at the 1993 Victorian Premier's Awards. He has been the recipient of a number of grants from the Literature Board of the Australia Council. He lives in the Blue Mountains outside Sydney.

Drift

BRIAN CASTRO

Published 1994 by William Heinemann Australia
a part of Reed Books Australia
22 Salmon Street, Port Melbourne, Victoria 3207
a division of Reed International Books Australia Pty Limited

Typeset in Sabon by Southern Cross Typesetting
Printed and bound in Australia by Australian Print Group

National Library of Australia
cataloguing-in-publication data:

Castro, Brian, 1950–.
Drift.

ISBN 0 85561 570 2.

I. Title.

A823.3

This work was assisted by a Writer's Fellowship
from the Australia Council, the Federal Government's
arts funding and advisory body.

for Jo

Preface

B.S. Johnson (Bryan Stanley Johnson, 1933–1973) was a little known though important British author who dared reassess the novel form. A true descendant of Samuel Beckett, he had earned praise from Beckett himself. Anthony Burgess wrote that Johnson's work was 'original ... in the way that *Tristram Shandy* and *Ulysses* are original', and Auberon Waugh nominated him for the Nobel Prize.

The reviewers thought differently ... mainly because they couldn't assimilate fact with fiction. For this was Johnson's challenge:

> Now anyone who wants simply to be told a story has the need satisfied by television ... Life does not tell stories. Life is chaotic, fluid, random; it leaves myriads of ends untied, untidily ... Telling stories really is telling lies ... I am not interested in telling lies in my own novels ... The novel is a form in the same sense that the sonnet is a form; within that form one may write truth or fiction.

To reviewers infected with Dickensian limitations, this was like a red rag to a bull. To this extent Johnson was shabbily treated by many of his literary contemporaries. Overcome by immense depression, perhaps on account of the death of his mother ('Em' or 'Emily'), he took his own life on 13 November, 1973, in London.

Before his death he had resolved to write a trilogy of experimental novels entitled: *See the Old Lady Decently, Buried Although,* and *Amongst Those Left Are You;* these titles to be read as one sentence across the spines of the books. At the time of his death, he had only completed the first volume.

In that book, the first of the 'Matrix' trilogy, he invited his readers to complete the other two volumes, as if through a prolepsis he had already planned his suicide. His obsession with mother, motherland and motherhood brought to his work a peculiar ambivalence about England and its imperial past. In a tiny passage he described what was unmistakably Tasmania.

This then, was a point of departure for me. It hung upon this thesis: that if Johnson declared that everything he wrote was the truth, then his obviously fictional works, his most defensively imaginative creations, would entail the complete fulfilment of his projections. This could only make for madness, but it also called into question the whole idea of commitment and responsibility:

> Compared with the writers of romances, thrillers, and the bent but so-called straight novel, there are not many who are writing as though it mattered, as though they meant it, as though they meant it to matter.

Thomas James McGann
Arthur River, 1993.

I

... and some of us still possess maps where the blanks are filled in with vague descriptions, but now we can sit and look comfortably at a photograph and know that our fellow-countrymen out there have settled down to a pleasant life under a fair sky.

Forest solitudes magnificent, glories of secluded fern-tree vales, 'England all over', untouched beauties, patched with the most lovely flowers and the most curious and elegant orchids, rich fields hedged with sweet briar or broom, handsome country houses with five-walled gardens, conservatories, forcing-houses and lawns. Perhaps no part of the world can show relatively so many old people.

There are no aborigines now left in the island.

B.S. Johnson
See The Old Lady Decently

II

Buried Although ...

Let me get to the point immediately: I've always wanted to compose my own obituary.

I don't mean to be vain, just a bit more generous than my critics. I possess that vast flood of abstract wealth the dying will suddenly offer. After all, when suicide is thumping at the gate you know the heart is seeking final repose. Yes, the writing of this tale will literally kill me ... fragmented misreadings floating out into the universe, never to return. Take your pick. Some will bend it to their own purposes; others ... well, who knows? ... will keep it behind the cistern.

In the First Century BC, just before the birth of Christ, Lucretius (yes, he who said quite rightly that when you're dead you're dead, a Saviour notwithstanding), called such rough usage *clinamen,* a corrective movement, a swerve from the original. Well, it's one of the hazards of putting things down: you no longer belong to yourself. All those acolytes clamouring at the gate.

Here, a few beans nevertheless. Do with them what you will.

Life isn't a book, take my advice. And yet I had wanted so much to become someone. No, not a famous novelist, but one who was true to the idea, someone who didn't feel the need. And nowadays at least, someone who was extinct. Words, of course, still erupt like lava and I will pause just long enough for a shave. Excuse me. Ah!

Not a shave after all.

Open the window. Quick.

All around I can hear hasty, muddled writers beating the backs of their imaginations, poor groaning beasts ... Here! Do us a favour and take the revolver, Fyodor.

I once said to my father, during a rare moment of youthful communication with him, that I had intentions of becoming a journalist. A journalist seemed to me to be always somebody, someone in work, at least.

I want to be in the newspaper business, I said.

Perhaps the word 'business' had been so alien to his working class roots that I involuntarily muffled it, contracted it, elided it.

I want to be in the newspapers.

My father turned abruptly and clouted me on the ear.

Now, don't you go doing anything stupid, you understand?

Well, I may still rate a brief column in the end. The magazine of which I'm currently the editor will at least make some appropriate noise, postmodern perhaps, having believed I was really dead all these years anyway. The life of an author is not an easy one. Biography is paradox: writing a life ... possibly oxymoronic. Their obituary, like my editorials, would weld itself together with contradiction. To have

Disappeared with a slight trace.

Antiseptic, devoid of resonance, you can see; the first sign of the end of mankind. Everything dies with me. It's really a matter of how much of myself I'm willing to put on the line ... the aura, corona, persona, fide bona ...

Enough of this posturing. I still write nothing but the truth.

Come to the moment ... the blow-torch ... maybe an explosion.

Well, her name was Emma McGann. Not a really exotic name ... didn't signal deep resonances, languid looks, sultry Italianate poutings, humid thighs. Signed without a flourish. A childish hand, really, though accomplished, and that attracts. She wrote telling me she liked my books. We exchanged pleasantries ... difficult for me, though I can vouch for extreme discipline in the formalities of writing ... deteriorating of course with age. A few cards whistling back and forth, hers cast in the native adornment of the Antipodes ... you know the kind of thing: manic pointillism and pithy runes all carrying some ancient, impenetrable secret (at least we managed to extinguish our dreamtime and invent psychoanalysis). She was Aboriginal. She had a twin brother. The difference between them, she wrote, was in colouring. They were descended from mixed parentage. Well, we wrote, and pretty soon I was falling in love (I fall in and out of love easily). Let me get one of her letters. Ah! Here she is. Imagine. It reads like a prophecy. Not yet ... too much reading and it goes stale.

And so ...

Whatever happened at Cape Grim?

Ah! Here you are, Emma.

I can see the soft plateau and the sheep tracks, the dung and the muttonbird burrows, the tussocky slope leading without warning to the precipitous cliffs and the sheer drop into the sea. I can see the Bass Strait winds blowing so fiercely you hang on for dear life to the long grass and pray the sea won't heave and swallow you up, you, growing dizzy lying on your back holding down your dress, watching the albatross glide in place, wings perfectly shaped to scoop up the wind which is scooping up your dress ... yes, how I can see that!

Gravity had drawn me to you. The gravity in your letters. I became tired of lies, of jokes, although you could have said I was defeated by honesty. That just about summed up my life: honesty was the boulder I pushed uphill. I refused to imagine. I was through with Grand Hotels, *Kathedernihilismus,* the abyss. The Latins, of course, derided gravity and invented angels, cherubic heads on wings which whirred out of grass trees and whittled the air. I can see you snapping their necks and carrying them home to the pot.

It's no good imagining, for it brings no comfort. Just creates another hole into which we fall, a temporary amnesia. The disease of mankind, imagining; it takes the place of forgetting, guilt, repression. Why have history otherwise, if not to celebrate the continuity served by ritual? Facts, not imagination, the latter all self-obsession. Think of the other. Her. Smell. She comes back. Your letters bordered with flowers, there the press of your palm. Quink. You wear no perfume, have an ancient hand, your phrases ornamented with the bouquets of the past.

I was in a state. Even without the imagination, coincidence dogged me to the extent my life had become a nightmare. Everywhere I turned I found the paradigm of a beginning, a middle and an end. Fabrication, false-consciousness, living-for-others. I couldn't breathe. My doctors said it was a kind of narcolepsy, hypnopompic states; a procession of words without sleep. Meaning swelled and heaved, it gave me headaches. In bed, my girlfriends used to tell me to do it myself: Byron, if you think your life is this bloody important, you've got your hand on the wrong bloomin' thing.

I suppose your letters were a kind of morphine, a narcotic with a reminder of underwritten pain, always accompanied by the shadow of an angel. They say when you feel wingbeats the end is nigh. Most though, feel nothing. Vacancy is the price of self-importance. I've seen great minds in nursing homes extracting trivia from final moments, with everyone taking notes. Reading your letters, a giddiness took hold. Prithee, draw me back a while.

New Year's Eve sometime in the 1820s.

Off the larboard bow they paid out the rode and launched the whaleboat. A creak here and there. Tonight they were going to bring back women. Aye, every man rum-drunk and erratic as muttonbirds. All imagining. Some in black-and-white, some in colour. Some only through smelling or touching. Pretty poor samples after spending years in sundry cages awash on deck or in mouldy holds, brains porous from poor diets of salt-pork and worm-eaten biscuits. They see women in conjunction with leg-irons, rum bottles, oakum, canvas and blubber. They stink in their slops, salt-chafing seams of their monkey jackets and flushing trowsers, greasy Scotch caps. They pull on the ash oars, the cold spray in their faces which all but whalers find healthy.

At the steering oar is Sperm McGann, who feels moved to issue a warning: Remember that these are cunning creatures we are capturing.

The two long-haired Aboriginal guides apparently not understanding long sentences.

I have always celebrated the intermittent, appended indiscretion and forgetfulness. That's how stories are formed. Ask the anthropologists. They mostly go backwards, as I once intimated as honestly as possible, but I guess we'll never know the truth, which lies in contradictory fragments. Put them together one way, like a jigsaw: make a story. Put them together differently: make another. As for you and me, I remember that summer when we fought honesty. I remember how we tried to rid ourselves of the stench of death by saying there would have been no funeral rites at Cape Grim, no morbid odour of coffinwood, just blood and bone leached back into the sea and the odour of dogs on heat. We invested the place with views, health, fresh-air monitoring stations, and cleaned up the stains of the past. It was that kind of summer, a summer of solitary beauty, enchantment and ultimately, terror. Well, if you let it get to you.

But wait. I must have known that in time a huge tide would erase everything. There was a sea-log which I'd marked with your letters. Damned if I know where I put it. Have to go below, destroy it. Excuse me. Otherwise the police will come aboard with their sniffer dogs and apprentice butchers, thirsting for postmortems.

Here it is, damp, expanding pages like a doughy concertina, edges lacy, fried with eggwhite. Open.

You were a blank page then. (Don't be upset. I'm not an engineer. I waited until you allowed me to describe you, until I knew that you knew. Perhaps this too was a violation.) It's a result of my inheritance, and yours too. The pen: the repository of so much weakness. The pen: a reminder of apprenticeship, failure to live, yet allowing only death to remain alive. Always too late. See this finger, this cold bunion of lost passions. Good only for ledger entries and classroom lesson plans and the filing away of faces. Unfolding now, this snake, this line which has become the relief of guilt, sounds like the scratching of genitalia, the rasping of graphite pubes. There's a vague hope there, without anyone else seeing. A peephole, a Judas-hole, nothing more. Which you helped me fill in.

Let me illustrate: I'm on a coach journey and the bus passes in and out of heavy rainforest and when it is dark outside, I see reflected in the glass the woman in the seat in front of me. I watch her legs, her short skirt, the way she puts her hands on her knees. I see her turn her hand to examine her fingernails. I watch her open her handbag, take out a receipt, add it up. I can count her money, which is loose in her bag, not folded away in her purse. There isn't much. She takes out a couple of smooth pebbles, rolls them around in her palm. I can study her rings. She has one on every finger of her left hand except on her thumb. Only a certain kind of woman wears a ring on every finger. I decide she is a woman of experience. I notice the black roots of her hair sprouting up from underneath the part that is dyed. A sweet profile, soft skin, eyes enigmatic, fluttering indecision. Then the bus comes out of the forest and light floods through the windows and the woman has disappeared. I long for her but am relieved at the same time. When the darkness returns so does she, and when we both alight, we carry an intimacy so intense it was as if I had made love to her. But all she has done is add up receipts and count her money. Seeing without searching, glancing without examining. That is how we love. It all depends on the dark ... on what we left out. And that was how I saw you, my dear Emma.

My name is Johnson. Full name? Byron Johnson. [Honestly though, it is Byron Shelley Johnson. (Romanticism ran deep in my mother, but what's in a name? At school I yearned for the embedded midnomer to be drowned out, to no avail; it sounded silly.) 'B.S.' is what my friends call me now, but it's a bit soon to take that liberty.] I change my name often to protect the innocent. I mostly write under the name of Johnson. Although someone is trying to start up the rumour that I write thrillers and detective novels and mutilation sagas under well-known pseudonyms, something like Kellerman or Harris, or the more praenominal Leonard. Leonard Johnson. Whoever it is, he or she is steering clear of Ben and Sam. I let it ride but it's normally against my nature. I'm obsessed by truth. But the truth is, nobody cares. Not one sleuth has tried to discover if we are all one and the same. Which does prove in a way that the author doesn't really matter too much.

In real life of course, I'm a bit of a bum. I try to be a good bum. No Porsches hidden in a lockup. My royalty statements littered with minus signs, even my minuscule advances retarded me.

Oh, and I'm looking forward to:

Chronic rheumatoid arthritis
Incontinence
Osteoporosis
Contractures
Fibrositis
Bronchitis
Hypertension
Rectal carcinoma
Paraphrenia

Inguinal hernia
Dementia
Et cetera

What's this? A liturgy? A fortune cookie? A prophylactic prayer? A Christmas list of antonyms? Superstition? Fate?

No, it's a journal ... and I'll have to force some writing onto it each day, which cannot be dissociated from any other ... parasitic days, symbiotic and sucking days indistinguishable from the profusions of disgust, loathing, anxiety, each day the last, except for this practice causing something to be set in motion ... shit, piss, the pen: the repository of so much weakness.

Indeed, of my latest book one notable critic said I should have won the Nobel Prize. Two of the greatest living writers labelled me 'original' and 'most gifted'.

In moments like these I would have liked to die.

I had them to dinner, bought expensive drinks, found nothing in common. Say no more. Except that my mother locked herself in the next room, coughing and whimpering, until they left.

I'm stuck in Hammersmith, London, SW13. I'm dying in Hammersmith, London, SW13, pretending my life was something else, and even though there's a kind of drudging discipline, an immitigably *English* drudgery, there's also a terribly overwhelming emotionalism. I needed love. (This too, was an English thing, to need but not to display ... screwing oneself up without help.) And by will, by force of will alone, was dizzily bending my life towards its irrationalities.

Then suddenly I was receiving letters from Tasmania. I felt dizzy again. The hole into the past gaped.

They ply towards shore, a mess of rock and shingle four hundred yards away. Cliffs loom, but nobody worries. They don't look at cliffs, just as they don't look at whales when they broach. Fright at the size makes one paralytic. 'Tis the deep casting an image, Sperm McGann said. Pull a whale ashore and 'tis no more fearful than a blubber raft.

At fifteen, slicing up ambergris in the belly of a beast, two flensers crackling with blood had held him down and violated him. The initiation, they said. You either get to like it or you fight it. McGann broadened his shoulders, furling sail and mincing whalebrain for spermaceti. His sharpened spade needed only four good strokes. He held up the blocks of wax. A record for a kid. He kneaded the substance. Shaped it into their faces. They were rather surprised, pleased almost. Hee haw. Within the belly of another whale, he decapitated them. Stuffed their testicles in their mouths.

Nobody messed with him after that.

It can happen anywhere, anytime. I have to sit down. Sometimes I'm gone for an hour, for a day. It's getting worse. I'm told amnesiacs discover whole new worlds, unknown galaxies, possibilities forever unaccounted and unaccountable, blank balance sheets; that they appear conscious only from one moment to the next, flickering, like an animal. Phenomenal. No wholes, no gelatinous presence, but sometimes profound sensitivity.

Yes, it's heartbreaking to return from such fugues to the cheap wisdom sniping at the air between these advertising hoardings, the batwings of my soul ... wisdom's sour breath as it grabs the back of my neck and thrusts me up against reality. Nothing there, between aspiration and my story ... a desire to tell, with an insufficiency of logic which I cannot even begin to explain.

But what if you, dear Emma, won't tell me more, allowing your pain to be locked within you forever?

Witness the reason for this shoal upon which I sport, ask why I look longingly at my own death with mucilaginous eyes, staring from a lost cove into one of the most isolated stretches of the mind. Oh, how I long to get away!

But you are keeping me from that. You, who harbour fear, perhaps a story which I have to know before I ... though if given a suicide, I hope you will be able to say: 'There goes commitment, there, the grist of understanding', and if you can say that now, then, dear Emma, let's drink a bottle together.

Why, then, do these tears still cling, if they're not reptilian? It's the sulphur in the air. They mine here in south Wales ... my holiday destination ... as far as I can afford. I wish I could come to Tasmania instead. The air stinks, the hills run with slag, the stream through the town belches a kind of black liquid. There's a STOP sign stuck in the mud, uprooted in some motor accident, which now bespeaks a prophecy if no one repents. Cold too. Icy flakes peel over fences.

At pre-arranged points, company buses pick up the men. They stamp in their overalls with lunch boxes in hand, queuing docile and grateful. The buses grind past, windows fogged with breath, heads lolling in sleep, oil smearing the panes. They don't see me. They don't see that I want to die for them.

But I'm on holidays.

In the mornings Mother slurps her porridge and sneers with a broken tooth.

Twelve novels published ... with each, the hole getting smaller, like on a sinking ship, water level closing off the escape hatch ... twelve novels and I still can't feed her. She lives off a pension and has done so for twelve years while I've been writing books from the day of Father's death. The day after, in fact, when I ransacked the house and sold the furniture.

So now the day wanes into an insipid glare. I'm tired of these venial ambitions, the mimicry of culture. Tonight I'll break something, shatter the festivity of these celebratory moments which bring on nausea. Another literary function upon which I will vomit.

Back to London on the six o'clock train. Words will be spoken. Arguments with well-fed men and women on private incomes all writing dull prose reeking with bad plumbing and afternoon tea-parties, extra-marital affairs and dubious heritage. Men and women who know nothing of the chaos of the soul, who are ignorant of the squeakings of real desperation.

A few of Ainslie's friends will be there and I'll find myself acting crudely, trying to squeeze a few quid out of them, knowing I'd have better luck with those who sleep under bridges. From the very beginning Ainslie and I agreed to have total freedom with each other's lives. She had a strange zeal, as aristocrats sometimes do, for saving the world. She disappeared every so often to Marrakesh, Zanzibar, Bangladesh. She was doing things for World Vision, Save The Children, Amnesty International etc., although I suspected there was something else behind it ... behind the network of women bureaucrats, late-night phone-calls, assignations, official dinners. Perhaps it was something as mundane as power. You could get a buzz out of the alms corporation, receive eleemosynary electricity or compassionate credit from hours of talk, reams of paper. The power to impose boredom.

Towards the end, when Ainslie and I separated, she used to accuse me of not adding to the economy. I told her I was a daily donor to the sperm bank of England, might even have been fertilising Royal ovaries. Nights I used to creep into her flat at Knightsbridge to unsuccessfully sniff out other men in her underwear.

Ainslie. She was about two hundredth in line to the throne. Why she married a bum I don't know; I suppose being a writer attracted a certain type. The communion of souls, wisdom, all that sort of shallowness a woman working simultaneously in the Stock Exchange and in the United Nations inexplicably experiences. Perhaps the massive contradictions made her simplify things. She cried a lot, but I could never find her soul. She read best-sellers with a gun under her pillow. She realised early that honest Fascism got rid of a lot of unnecessary turmoil. I'm sure she had a hand in several revolutions. I was naïve enough to believe that had its attractions. She had no time. But for me, the wingèd chariot had turned into an agonisingly slow pendulum.

We parted amicably enough, after a long series of emotional tearings ... once you hit the motorway of bitterness you drive your separate ways forever ... though the signs say WRONG WAY! GO BACK! you gleefully wait for the fatal collision ... one irretrievable step at a time. We parted when numbness had made me invisible, socially inept even with my poetic dog-tag. After countless empty evenings at one function or another, I, who was always slow to shuffle my words and views, my Thames-side accent wandering rudderless in the upper reaches, became garrulous and outrageous. One night, after a dinner party with an ambassador and his girlfriend, after I had the girl's stockinged foot twitching like a landed fish in my crotch beneath the table, Ainslie and I began a violent argument. Later in the kitchen, she had picked up a fruit knife. I was insulted.

At least use a carving knife! I screamed.

She had completely forgotten the gun.

But Ainslie was not spiteful. Even as the removalists came, she was still throwing things my way. Using her influence, I became a judge on the Booker Prize Committee for literature. I picked up the books from the Hammersmith P.O., three big boxes of them (somehow it fell upon me to distribute duplicate copies to the other judges) and threw them into the river.

You sure you don't want any? Mother slurps, the tassels on her tea-cosy cap skimming the scum. With memories like these I won't cry at her funeral, unless the moment overtakes me.

New Year's Eve tonight in south Wales. Mother has lost her mind and the Welshmen are singing, but we won't be celebrating. Mother always switches off the lights at eight. You don't try to change that kind of routine. Except she suddenly says, looking at my lined pages stained with rinds of whisky: What are these circles for? Are they runes?

Everything is significant for Mother. It's the same with art. I'm tired of art. I'm simply celebrating quietly.

In our rented terrace in the Rhondda, I ladle out porridge from the aluminium saucepan, its handle glued to a florid tea-towel. I cut triangles of bread, bounce on some rubbery cheese and fire up the griller. Mother pulls down her knitted pot-warmer. It's three degrees in the kitchen. Food stains mark the side of the stove. Between the plastic sugar bowl and the greasy tin teapot, there is a hole in the wall made by mice. A peephole.

Off to London tonight, then away, never to return. My mother will die, kill herself out of anger and remorse. There'll be a murder tonight, I guarantee. But first, the peephole. It's where I keep Emma's letters, just in case Mother comes across them. She would have no qualms about reading Royal mail. Damn. My cheese-toast is burning. Smells like blubber.

Sperm McGann went a-whaling and when there were no ships for him, drifted along the quays of Hobart Town, notorious in the 1820s for its stink of try-works, melted blubber hanging heavy in the drizzle. It was notorious for other things too, and McGann covered the waterfront, making waxworks, a dab hand at casting your simulacrum. Death crowded into his tent on the pier and sat for him. Outside, the freak shows, the Tiger Children, the Native Woman Born of a Whale, flesh carved like scrimshaw. In the pubs and laneways, murder, rape, a commerce in dried heads.

They ply for shore, oars like the legs of a water spider.

Cadence, men.

McGann, master of his own whaleboat.

Lay aft!

Turning his head he sees the captain standing by the running lights, a flaring match over his pipe. The lines of the cliffs grow distinct. Rocks and inlets appear, sluiced sand peeping white, strands of pebble in the vague moonlight.

He steers the boat into a cove and smells the buttongrass on a shift of dead wind.

Ease oars!

They ground in the sand and drag the boat up, making sucking sounds with their feet as they reach in, gathering harpoons, spades, muskets, pistols, clubs. McGann motions to them and they follow. He knows this headland like the back of his hand, his hand which is tattooed with scars and laced with tendons. He stoops, signals to avoid the twigs, branches, stones balanced on rocks — all the traps set for inferior ears — but he knows they would already have heard these white men, clumsy bastards, let alone smell them. He would have been concerned if not for the covenant he'd struck: axes for women. Move. Wait. Had to go through this charade like wombats. The natives expected it.

In the next cove, a red glow. Around it, sleeping figures, one turning, slapping at a mosquito. An incandescent log splits and explodes ...

Aaiiieeegh! A roaring. Bloodlusting. Men charging on top of others. The sound of steel upon flesh. Confusion. No form to this but naked power. An old man lifts his head and receives a musketball which snaps it back and bone and brain spray out in fountains of blood. We respect no covenant, McGann yelled, bearing down with supposed courage and alcoholic pride, while three young men stand with trembling spears, cut down with harpoons before they can aim. Aaiiieeegh! Human flesh is nothing to such fine lances and practised arms, the expanding barbs clean through the other side. Children clubbed like seal pups. In five minutes they are dragging the women with them, pushing them into the whaleboat, the natives running off in smoke and swirling firebrands, gurgling with blood while their brothers are hoisting them on shoulders without seeing McGann's men return to finish them off, muskets like bursting flowers, cascading sparks in their backs which are suddenly wet and dark and the woman McGann holds in a headlock has smoke in her hair, frizzled fish-oiled hair smelling like smoked salmon.

Opening a tin of kippers for lunch, I marvel at how these far reaches keep cropping up, but I won't have history yield to mere imagination. I'll have to go to Tasmania, put the pieces together, abandon writing to disprove the artefact. In London they are already making a mockery of me. Witness this unkindest cut; the usual journalistic canard of reducing literature to patriotism:

> He really should get out of Britain. His 'innovatory technique' is nothing but young wine in old bottles, a kind of puritanical confession in rebellion against the imagination, which he classifies as 'lying'. It just doesn't cut the mustard here. We're a nation of craftsmen, not noted for experimentation and anarchy, for those Continental practices of public self-humiliation, microscopic recordings of self-consciousness and irresponsible frivolity. All this is more of the same really, but in the final analysis, writing is writing, life is life ... and the former is always subordinate to the latter.
>
> *The London Review of Books*

Pure tabloid. Mark my words: even my death will be a failure.

I worm past slag heaps searching for a pint of Welsh bitter, lukewarm, hopping amongst the crippled and desperate, the victims of mine disasters, little bent-over men with lung diseases, the spittle slippery underfoot even after they shovel on the sawdust.

Why drag my old mother here for a holiday?

At the age of ten they evacuated me to Wales while she was bombed in Hammersmith, pieces of aircraft and human debris and shrapnel landing on our greenhouse, our little glass shed in our tiny backyard where my father used to grow spring onions. Smells like roast pork, Mum said, looking up, until pieces of entrails smeared her specs.

Yes, I was removed to south Wales and placed with a family, he a locomotive driver for the mines, having spent most of his life in India; she from Rajasthan, a little woman who cooked chutney and mixed pickles and lime all day, telling stories of India as she cooked. Despite all the brutality of those times, she had focussed her life on spices, and despite this terrible war against the Germans, had made each little rationed meal as delicious as a feast with her home-grown herbs, making my mouth water (indeed, I remember now ... it was the slowness with which we were required to eat, masticating twenty times before swallowing, chillies and herbs infusing my nasal passages with fiery snuff which bonded with the word ... *delicious* ... arrggh! ... *delicious* ... water! ... the paradoxes of taste ... the next day wishing I could have shat in a bidet), as I now walk past the slag-filled river, the cold wind biting, tearing through the valley, almost smelling her meal-time commands and stories and bringing my old mother here to share what only I am appreciating ... another woman's cooking. A true family, they were. Dead now, the locomotive driver and his wife, but I can still smell chutney and pickles above the sulphur and coaldust. It is emanating from *Pertab's Punjabi Pop-In Place* up the street. Pertab's son a mining engineer with gambling debts.

So, into the curry-house.

Hello, Pertab, you old perturbaned Punjabi.

Hello and how's your father?

Neither of us knows each other well. Ethnicity and confusion in practice here. Unfortunate, this mention of my father. I normally apologised for the luxury of eating out. I let it be known my father left us for a fancy woman and got knifed in Shanghai. Years later the communists paid up for the liquidation of his business, so we cashed in his shares. It wasn't enough, but I've got these credit cards, you see. Lies buy time. What could I have said? That my father, this country, my years of national service owed us these slag heaps, this curry, this lukewarm beer?

Nobody owed anybody anything.

They didn't take credit cards in the Rhondda.

My father was in the First War. See this photo of him, a portly man with a pipe, a pudgy face, kindly, almost.

He was at Ypres and came back. One of the few. Gassed. Emphysema gave him that gurgling in his lungs. He said he was glad he wasn't an officer. I hasten to add there was no bullet-hole in his back. The working class had its advantages, nothing to live up to, but nothing to die for. He and a mate shot their lieutenant before they went over the top.

He gave me this gold-nibbed dip pen he said he'd taken from the body of a dead German ... an officer. Then later, when he was dying, he said the German gave it to him.

I told him it was all right, my father said. I told him that everything was all right, and of course it wasn't all right. His guts was oozin' out weren't it? It was a lie. It weren't even a comforting lie. I should've told him he was dying. That's when he gave me the pen ... for me to write to his family. It is my experience that people never carry out the wishes of the dying. Have you still got the pen son?

Yes, Da.

Write honestly with it.

Yes, Da.

I can understand now, the emotions which must have coursed through my father ... the curse of not being able to be alone, always in bars and nightclubs, dreaming the ideal love-affair, always with feral women, his imagination playing ninety-five per cent of the parts, inventing nostalgia, grief and triumph ... how he must have suffered, not being able to write these things down, having lost his right arm at Ypres, and always, at the end of it all, the terror of loneliness.

Nobody owes anybody anything.

I taught this to my pupils. For years, in London, I was in Supply. They drew me from a pool and I spent my days calling the roll and counting lunch money, starving kids hanging off me, Sir, Sir, I got no fork'n knife!

Don't swear, son. It's not nice.

At London University, attending night-time lectures, I learned about extinction. Unicorns, native Tasmanians, the frenzy of purity and cleansing during nationhood. I was excited. Immortality, I thought, was made of this: perilous nativity, tough titty, no spilt milk and revenge. I was fascinated by what pioneers called *woolly-haired savages.*

My Latin tutor thought differently. A kindly man, Julius Jenkins hunched over dusty volumes of Virgil in an ivy-choked room, his pipe challenging newly-installed fire regulations. Jules thought the end was near for all of us. In a murky pub in the East End he put his hand on my knee. We are all unicorns, he whispered. We bring maidens to the world and are slaughtered for our sensitivity.

I ate my stew and drank the lukewarm lager. A callow youth, I was surprised that poetry was all we had. I wasn't interested in myths and muses. Give me the Tasmanians any day. I grew dizzy with the possibilities; thought of succumbing to the falling-down disease and suddenly, memory fused. In those days my fits went nowhere. I sometimes saw myself dreamt and written by another:

Byron Johnson used to ride his bicycle to the school in which he taught, excited continuously by women: students, teachers, office staff. It was a better reason to keep going than his meagre salary. He was big, nervous; he looked as though he was about to thump you on the back; yet he carried deep within, a massive, debilitating romanticism. It was aching, unmentionable, and he kept it hidden, having learned from experience that in sunlight it was mocked ... he was familiar with the agony, with its ability to turn him hard upon himself like a beetle upon its back. Witness a normal day:

He parks his bike, locks it with a chain, climbs upstairs with his rucksack full of books. He pauses near the book-room, a musty cupboard of a room with one cell-like window, jammed with shelves of half-used texts, torn, faulty bits of education delivered daily to bored and needy pupils. Pauses there because he has the only key and listens to the sounds therein, surprised. A woman moans, in the semi-darkness, the unmistakable tones of the new American teacher and her Science Master, both married and illicit, limned in dust-motes, kids staring through the broken pane from above. He goes on upstairs and will return later to sample the frenzied air, juxtapose the bookish spoor with musk and semen.

Always have to test for reality.

He was too delicate for this job. He employed great formality towards the American, inoculating his lust with contempt, holding her chair to receive her toothy charms ... Americans appreciate old manners ... admiring her capacity for rough passion and the unconscious gentleness it produced, but he didn't once correct himself to consider the effects of being too ruthless in this search for evidence.

Rode my bike to school one day and the Science Master, great bull of a man who'd done some wrestling in Bromwich, said: I have a car space right? An' you bloody well go an' park your bike there. That's not the way we do fings 'ere, right?

So the next day I parked my bike on top of his car and at lunch he found out and wanted to fight me then and there, masticated food gushing from his mouth, but others held him down and he calmed, the whole school watching in silence and then in giggles. The incident made me trim some fat, but it did no good because a week later he tried to run me down along High Street and I couldn't pedal fast enough and ended up through the bamboo blinds of a curry shop. On another day, a friend of his who drove for Cherry's Meats side-swiped me, the lorry catching one of my pedals and I was dragged sideways up a hill.

I quit teaching. I'd had enough aggravation.

It was then that I met Ainslie.

Coincidentally, in the bank in which I worked.

This was after I had sold all the books in my possession, had made up my mind that the humanities were redundant in an age of debit and credit. There was a terrible weight within my chest, I couldn't breathe half the time, lugging the weight of failure from room to room, such was the anger, and I longed for that day I would hold up a grenade or a stick of dynamite, pull the pin or light the fuse and sit there for the final absorbing seconds.

For one moment he'd dreamt the past and saw how far down he'd come. To think that the first novel at twenty-five had brought such acclaim he believed he'd go on forever, forgetting what he had so often written about: that fame was the attrition of that isolated world in which the best was always produced. It was the bitter amber of commonality which destroyed him; yes, quite paradoxically it had made him into a type. They took him for granted. He was furniture. Sooner or later, the brief editorship of an unknown magazine and then the fight against poverty; alcoholism. Noblesse oblige. No vulgar daytime jobs. He went under. Begged in pubs. With a final monumental effort, through the help of his old tutor Julius Jenkins, he got the job in School Supply. And now, scrubbed up, a bank Johnny catching the eye of a blonde girl. He was smiling. Had some vague notion of her smart clothes, silk scarf and all the expensive accoutrements.

These attractions passed, more or less rapidly. The eye becomes jaded within the orbit of bitterness. With training and effort, I could have developed contempt, but the defences were down. There was this other side to me. Genius, Einstein said, was energy. $E = MC^2$. I looked busy. Stepped from behind the counter to refill the deposit slip holders. She was close to me, completing a form. Subtle perfume. When she reached across for a pen she said Excuse me and her breast brushed my arm and then the pressure became firmer, and she said: I seem to know you, perhaps I've seen you before?

And I said I don't believe so, running through my list of brazen breasts.

It was only later that they told me this was her father's bank.

Yes, she insisted, not here. On the BBC. You're some sort of comedian.

Not bloody likely. I smiled instead at her, with feigned ignorance.

There it was. See how the briefest of dialogues interposed itself and took root, when normally, in the coarse commerce of life these phatic sounds were erased in daily sleep after a second's scintillation. But there it was. The bloody thing came out like a snake from its hole ... the correction, erratum, arrogance, flawed pride and false modesty of the writer. Oh precious little excitement! Another piece of integrity down the drain. Byron Shelley. The writer of a dozen 'novels', if you believed in the new; you couldn't call contemporary epistles new; proselytisers, poetasters, panegyrists who make up the litcrit crowd couldn't abide the new; old wine in new bottles, they called it, which is always a change. We're talking quality. Byron Shelley Johnson. Revolutionary. Hard enough as it is to hold my names together in anonymous penury. We Johnsons were good bums. We had an American branch ... who came originally from Hammersmith ... old winos. They knew how to use their Johnsons.

So that was when it all began. I signed her copy, which she had promptly bought at a nearby store, and then made an entry in my diary:

Enterprise = Mindless romance + Chronic boredom^2.

That was what my life was worth. Nothing was beyond its recording. But for now, things were looking up. Ainslie liked slumming. These were the days before art had stock-market cachet. It wasn't so unusual. From time immemorial the rich had taken genius from the gutters and destroyed it completely. It was more dangerous with writers. Paintings didn't bite back. I didn't know why she was interested. It could never have been pity.

And yet I was not loveless. If you could have seen me revolve on the dance floor, the shabby halls I frequented, nights of perspiring girls fleetingly beneath, but each, a narrative, the orb in its motion like an angel singing, as the bardic breath whistled it. Living on onions and garlic then. Until one, Priscilla her name, so desperately drug-riddled her brain almost porous, walked straight through the thin glass door of my bathroom and stood clutching her jugular, unmoving, and collapsed then, in pulsings of arterial blood, and when I carried her to Casualty, to the old Hammersmith Medical Building in which my birth had been registered, she had become cold and heavy in the shrouded night, and I believe things reached me from the other side, each bottle of infused blood, each sputtering of deathly breath, each clank of stainless steel, poured cheap wisdom into me, the sanctity of life found so often in careless harmony with ephemera ... a pulse or two, and then infinity ... and what had generated it was like a snap of air.

And then there was Linka the Czech, who was escaping a man with no past, Jimmy Jeans, his name. She had him checked out, so to speak, and found a list of crimes so long the police were interested suddenly and didn't leave her alone until she'd confessed he held a knife to her throat and this gave them cause for an arrest: of a leathery addict who never changed his trousers. But it was always the haunting refrain that he had no past which worried her, as if he would slip out of gaol one day like wind between the bars and she would hear him whistling on the landing, no sex, no sex, as though he were afraid, but in reality making the long association with murder by chastity. He killed prostitutes. And Linka was his only love, provided she was Mother.

I bought a cut-down .22 from the dealer across the street, filed the numbers and honed the stock to a stained haft which neatly fitted my hand, but by that time Linka had gone, leaving behind her perfumed loneliness, the same I'd smelled that second time I met Ainslie Cracklewood at Stromboli's, where I was working as a waiter.

She came in with two other women, blonde, you could have said clones, and ordered expensive cocktails. She ignored me at first, and then asked if I had ever been a comedian, for I looked so sad. A good joke. Then, quite drunk, she began to hum tunelessly and on the way to the Ladies' Room, cornered me by the phone-booth, saying I should resign.

She may need some filling in: you can imagine ... dimples, immaculate teeth but flawed blue eyes, drowning peacock-blue eyes, you could have said, but in reality unfocussed, short-sighted, unused perhaps to contact lenses, her cheeks afire. I admired her nerve but not her style, and she was holding herself very straight, royally so, though her words were tumbling about. I told her I had to support my poor old mother. That was when she stuffed £200 into my apron and kissed me. You write that, she said. And I must admit it was a different kind of kiss from those of the small number of women I'd kissed before, because it was so tentative after her making the running and all that, and I thought maybe she hadn't really done much of this before ... that is, pick up a waiter who was really a writer, though it was the same, waiting is what writers do, waiting for something which may never come, the end, the beginning, the truth or nothing ... waiting for words which are spent and for which one has nothing to show. No, it was a kiss from a novel if ever there was one, not like those I'd known from women who had dirty feet and pimply backs, who left saliva on your chin and sought no more than peace with a bloke, the attendant happiness of romances they read in bed, so unlike themselves, books whose plots were written purposefully with planned direction and cunning ... women who drifted, and were real.

You have to have peace in order to write, Ainslie said.

Nothing I have heard since has been further from the truth. So, after a few drinks I took myself up to meet the challenge, took her up on it, or rather she took me up, or I took up with her and what with all this taking up with each other, I didn't see Stromboli approaching with two heavies, didn't feel his hot breath behind, but certainly heard his warning: You're a fuckin' fool, Byron Johnson.

Be that as it may, Ainslie and I connected in a way that was different from any other relationship I've had before or since: we were driven by a common hatred of complacency. We goaded each other on. I reflect now on the strenuousness of that courtship; all that imaginative effort evolving into nothing.

Stromboli tore the apron off me and threatened violence, but Ainslie's friends intervened and at the mention of a name or two, caused Stromboli to blink. It took a little while, but then we all seemed to be moving in slow motion, until the instinct for corruption took hold. Stromboli became as nice as pie and gave us drinks on the house and we all parted amicably, the clones in Stromboli's Roller and Ainslie and I to her apartment in Bloomsbury, where she said I could either spend the night in her bed or on the couch, or in the Tube station, if it were that important to preserve decorum. Please yourself, she said, but let it be known she understood excess perfectly.

Ten years in Supply and I'd almost forgotten women's bodies. In Ainslie's bed I thought of my mother, arthritic, storing up tinned food for me in case of her passing. She hobbled desperately and fumbled with the tea things at four o' clock, her once perfect knees nobbled with elastic tights to contain her falling, her mad flights wheeling and skating towards the fire and ice of Ultima Thule, she in her blank year, cast adrift from history. Byron, don't fall for cat-women, she said, all that piss and smell and perfumed thighs. I'd rather you'd caught a boat for South America.

And at this point never failed to hold out banknotes, scarcely enough for soup.

Ainslie held out for nothing. Her nightdress unruffled, puritanically commissioned, she employed a standard repertoire and then apologised. Sorry, didn't give you half a chance. You can improve on that in the morning.

Ten years in Supply and I was still a romantic.

Lust repeated led to chaos. Ainslie was confused as to why I had no passion, didn't pursue her across town, spy on her assignations, drift along icy streets, shoes caked in slush, or wait in panting taxis. She half wished, she said in an unguarded moment, I would trap her in an alleyway, lift up her skirt and take liberties. Oh fuck, she said, are all writers the same? Words and nothing but words?

I lied to Mother. Said I was going to Stromboli's each morning, but went to the apartment and hung about till noon, reading, drinking Turkish coffee and listening to Mozart while Ainslie slept, then quietly left when she woke, regularly at two.

Ainslie had other men. Sex is not possession, she said, and I agreed. I wasn't drawn to her for that. One day, the boyish, foppish Lord _____, who was always appearing in the tabloids and who affected a monocle, hung around with me outside her door. When it became apparent that she wasn't there we went and bought each other a pint and didn't mention Ainslie once. We spoke about football, I about the innate talent of the working class, he about buying a club. He gave me the impression he was confused, and as it turned out, not about the club but about me. A waiter, he repeated; an accounts clerk; a schoolteacher. As for me, I wondered why he had been lining up outside her door, kicking at the carpet and pressing the lift button like a conscript awaiting a medical. According to Fleet Street, he was a fierce rake.

Ainslie must have affected all of us. She would try one thing and then another. She was full of ideas about changing the world. Most of her friends came from left field. I don't know where she picked them up. They always ended in business suits, publishing magazines she'd financed. She had an immense talent for seeking out the most important ingredient in people who could further her reputation, something she could learn, appropriate, use as currency. When she finished, she would let you go ... but not before you got a taste for champagne, the smell of luxury cars and the feel of silk underwear. Most of the time she demonstrated a particular tenderness for the anonymous and the disadvantaged ... she picked them off the streets ... because there she was able to hold herself above, remain intact and play with paradoxes. The poor had no such choices. Still, it was philanthropy of a sort.

Lord _____ confided this to me upon our second meeting. We were standing in the rain, in a rather grimy street near Madame Tussaud's. He'd accosted me and wanted an exchange of confidences, but I made excuses and hurried away. What he said about Ainslie didn't worry me. Besides, I thought, there was nothing to be gleaned from me. Books came in a flurry of circumstance and words accrued and sooner or later there would be a gentle snowfall of narrative, soft as shit. I fought hard for integrity, and wrote only what I knew. I despised the rococo, the arabesque and other writers, who tomorrow will always become someone else. That was human nature. I hated that too.

Ainslie and I must have loved each other once. It's difficult now to recall the emotion. Psychoanalysts used to call it the obscure object of desire, a lack, an invisible little thing. Maybe it was her freckled hands or the way she used her eyes or the ironic shape of her mouth. I can always tell a memory lapse is coming. We must have felt an extended longing, a wish never to be parted. It would have been chemistry at first. Oh, how I have even now to manufacture that first kiss! She must have been masterful in redefining happiness for me. She must have told me she admired the Herculean battles I fought each day, wrestling with honesty and perfection. Don't think, she whispered, when we made love. Don't feel you have to intellectualise. It was terrible flattery and wonderful consolation at the same time.

I must have been a working class boy with startled eyes. I suffered immensely from everything, life welling up like tears, unspoken, strangled. I made the sign of words, with my hands up to my mouth. That's how it had to be. We must have gone through a horrendous wedding, drunk from morning till night on champagne, her father jealous and irate to see a daughter go, but happy he had five sons to keep titles and fortunes secure. It still pains me a great deal to think about it.

Mother didn't show. She had a turn and re-occupied her hospital room. When I visited the next day, she asked me if I knew that people's noses continued growing until they died.

That Cracklewood girl's got a terrible snoz, she said. Tilts upwards. You can't trust toffs.

One night a few months into our marriage, Ainslie confessed that men simply didn't satisfy her. At least Englishmen. It came out in the course of our conversation, my post-coital distraction prompting such barbs, perhaps my leafing through anthropological texts while she worked at herself, when she revealed that men were a marauding species who had their place, but who were unable to understand the immense, oceanic largesse manifested purely by womankind. She breathed audibly. Her golden curls trembled.

Women communicated with each other, she said. Problems were talked out. Women ... *expressed.* Men simply sulked. How could she put up with it? It was clearly a critical moment. Premature. Out of control. Even your death will be premature, she said. Oh, no, she was not disillusioned, she merely wanted to cut some slack.

When she said that, I knew she had really rehearsed this well. Ainslie had twice failed on the stage. Once when she broke a leg in an amateur production, falling into the prompter's box because of her poor eyesight, and then with poor foresight had married a critic, Humphrey Eglington, who presided over the Booker committee. Divorce soon followed. Cutting some slack was one of her lines. I was next. The amazing thing was that it happened so reasonably. Love could be so strange. The end of it even stranger.

I care about you, she said, propping herself on an elbow, but I cannot stay in love with you. I've given you ... us ... the best chance possible, the colour rose in her cheeks ... but you've turned to stone, Byron. Even your work is lapidary. Time has passed you by, yet you want to get the present out of the way so you can get on with your work. I'm sorry. Perhaps I've been too equivocal. I just don't like being disappointed. Men are all the same.

It was a terrible Dear Johnson, especially for a writer. I thought of the tabloid headlines: *Royal thespian turned lesbian throws out B.S.* In the sheets I dug out a monocle which had been aggravating my back. Affixing it to my right eye, the one weak from imagining Sapphic delights, I noticed that she had a map tacked to the wall. Some sort of island shaped like a codpiece. I knew that Ainslie was a good liar, one of the very best, but this time she was really going to the ends of the earth to find an excuse. There was an issue here. Oh, I admit, things were never wonderful with me. I wasn't as exciting as she may have wished; didn't write a best-seller, take drugs or run after other women to make her jealous; ate peas off my knife before threatening her with it, that sort of thing. I believed in traditional ways and I couldn't behave differently with her. It must have been a class thing. I liked to roll my sleeves up; dismantled diesel motors in order to write about mechanics; built an indoor toilet for my mother to save on the plumbing ... wrote a novel about that too; still grieved for my father though he had never been good to any of us (spun that out for three novels); sat in pubs enjoying the dialect of seedy eastenders (turned that into a monologue for the BBC). But I still respected wealth and power. Not to reproduce but to experience. Furthermore, I wasn't as famous as Ainslie had believed. I was devastated. But I moved out the next day.

You really need to get out of Hammersmith, she said to me a few weeks later after we had parted amicably and when we allowed old habits to half swell up again.

I was there collecting my privately printed poems, reading from: *First Works: The Mangrove Mind,* by Shelley Johnson. It could still be exciting.

I can't leave my old mother.

She has you by the balls, Byron.

My time hasn't come.

Jesus, darling, they've got to fuckin' drop sometime.

I yawned, pretended to study the map again, but my heart had already shipped anchor, my early training standing by me, telling me to keep my distance. Then a kind of vertigo overtook me, I don't know why, perhaps from so much repression ... when there was so little time.

The brig rode at anchor. When the whaleboats turned upon the stroke of midnight ... although no one but the Captain knew it was midnight, he alone being in charge of time in these southern latitudes ... it was 1824 and it was damp and cold and frightening ... you can imagine: black water sweeping in from the south, antarctic winds whistling with the cold, fish washed up, the death-smell mouth of winter, and if your eyes were adjusted to the darkness you would've seen McGann and his men draw alongside, the three captured women whimpering at the bottom of the whaleboat, prodded up the swaying rope ladder, while at the rail McGann would've turned towards the others saying: *Let no one o' you touch this creature,* grasping the girl's hair and giving her head a shake, the men looking away and smirking, some farting in acknowledgment, all back-handed compliments to McGann's skilful woman-handling because the others wouldn't like this, the women back on the Great Island who had seen him come out of a whale's belly, had seen him standing in the blubber floating just off-shore covered in blood and oil, an iron paddle in his hand, and who had held to this vision of him as the Great Provider and had made him their common husband.

In the master-cabin, beside a candelabra supporting pots of smoking oil, Captain Orville Pennington-James sits depressed. A large man with a pigtail, he looks like a brooding hog except for the pallor and the wire spectacles and the smelly longjohns and the terrible sensitivity sitting heavy in his chest which had dogged him all these sailing days since he missed his calling to Harvard.

Pennington-James loves the sea. He is obsessed with navigation. He loves to pass his hand over wood, testing the chine of a single-beam cutter, setting his eye along the teak of a racing-class yawl. In the Massachussets Yacht Club, of which his father was president, Indian maids served hot toddies on foggy evenings, and when the horn moaned at midnight, he was often found swooning between pages in the quilted amber light of the stuffy library, a brahman before his time, while his father, aboard a moored schooner, burrowed between the legs of Pocahontas. The waitresses were all called Pocahontas and they charged mightily for simple favours. Pennington-James knew about the rough desires of men of a certain age. There was a lot to prove when the old bull faltered and his father became increasingly irritable.

You know nothing of the world, he said to his son. You won't survive, even amongst the feeble-wristed.

But despite this and a knowledge of the sea's indifference, he asked to be commissioned and set about proving that a marriage between practicality and sensitivity was possible. But all he had proved since was that his father was right: he was a danger to himself. Take that fellow McGann, a natural boatswain, not officer material, no decency there, but a natural leader just the same. He had the cunning look of a diviner. Yes, McGann's half-smile was going to be a bother to Pennington-James; he remarked on this the first time he set eyes on him, when the latter signed aboard. And now he has let this smart Billy, as they say in these waters (BIL.LI; Aboriginal: *buttock*), talk him into letting the men try sealing on these rocky coasts and windswept islets off Van Diemen's Land.

It was true that they had only caught one whale between Valparaiso and Sydney, but it was out of season. In Sydney, Pennington-James had picked up a dubious crew when his own men signed aboard a vessel bound for China. Their lay had come to very little. All the way from Nantucket, the Chief Mate had only managed eighteen dollars and he wasted no time urging the others to transfer. McGann and his group were a scurvied lot, given to drink, but they looked, for all that, able to catch a whale or two.

It had been a mistake from the very beginning.

Feckin' terrible, wrote Pennington-James in the log.

The watches were lazy, asleep, insolent when wakened, and every time a whale broached, looked the other way ... can you imagine? A feckin' five-tonner slapping down beside the Nora *so close you could taste krill in your mouth and these boneheads look at one another and say: Jaysus, was that a creature from the deep? And they scratch their bums and I withhold their provisions ... no whale no quail, which I have, in three barrels, preserved in rum, shot by my daddy hisself, then of a sudden, covering the wind off New Zealand we launched a boat and McGann, son-of-a-gun, stuck it and it sounded fifty fathoms, running the line out between my feet ... yes, I wanted action that bad ... and I came for'ard to pierce its heart but had a coughing fit from all that water in the lungs, my feet tripped by the line and then the water grew black and the boat lurched and the beast came up behind, black and shiny and stove the boat, flukes catching the steerer and I heard his bones crack, this fine crackling above the roar and the tumult of the churning water and suddenly I found myself kicking at barnacled blubber, the cetacean slewing, rolling, diving, making off for another attack and my spectacles were gone, I was swallowing water now, nothing beneath, so cold, the water in those latitudes, when I saw McGann hacking at the heavy rope with a spade, hacking at the blocks and he cut through finally and the boat wallowed and sucked and soon, upturned, the waves were breaking over all of us clinging onto the keel until the Second Mate's boat came to our assistance.*

Well, that was the last time I made it out in a whaleboat. They brought the injured man aboard, bones out through his flesh. The men refused all duty after the steerer died, did nothing, until three days later I thought up the brilliant tactical manoeuvre of making McGann whalemaster.

Well, the old brig lumbered on. Her bottom oozed and needed coppering. She stank, was too small for sperm whaling and could only melt down one or two whales at a time. As a foreign vessel she was forbidden in the bays. The men, ex-convict rabble-rousers sank back into their old ways, parochial bullying, corn-holing and drunken stupidity, of which they were inordinately proud ... all except McGann, who I could see was standing apart, scrutinising the main brace and watching for the main chance. He came in one morning and suggested leasing the ship as a sealer.

She would turn more profit in a season, he said, and you could sit counting the pelts.

He had that feckin' leer on his face. On paper it sounded good, the brig running up to Canton and Shanghai, where pelts were in high demand, but I couldn't put pen to paper then, having lost my spectacles in the previous mêlée. Besides, it had been a challenge, and I wanted yet to master this whaling thing. I wrote my father. I wanted to get it right, I told him. He knew a lot about this game. But my father had no time. His energies were then absorbed in running a string of brothels.

Pennington-James sits depressed. His father had taught him how to chase whale. Sealing's fer losers, his daddy had said, an' if you think that small you end up feckin' sardines.

His father's hairy forearm around his neck.

For one irrational moment he longs for milk, warm, creamy, straight-from-the-cow milk.

In the sweltering hold, McGann baptises his new beauty with stinking bilge water. Hush, he coos, running his wet hands over her startled eyes. Thou'rt a wondrous face indeed.

Though she was quite naked, save for some small private fetish of plaited vine, he didn't touch her further. He locked her in the lazaret, flicked his thumb at the sailor idling by the pumps and shut the connecting door. Then he went into his cabin and plunged his hand into a cauldron of hot rubbery wax, drinking in its odour. Presently rain pattered on the deck and this brought him to himself, pain inscribed on his arm. There was only the work, he was saying, as he peeled off the wax ... the work that I have yet to do, he said, some divinity caught in his memory. For he was going to record the evanescent faces of these strange and wily creatures.

So now for the six o'clock train to London. This, of course, will be a test ... the classic existential case of mother-indifference; treason perhaps, a weaning with no meaning, Mersault sans mercy. I can foresee the remorse of hindsight. I'll pay for casting off the motherland, for weighing anchor, becoming unhinged, taking my chances on the open sea.

Mother has cancer. When she finds out I've gone for good, she'll probably kill herself in that Welsh guesthouse. Nothing very dramatic, or quick. Simple malnutrition with complications. Or overdose by oversight. There's the huge bottle of morphine I've left in the fridge. My usual forgetfulness. I could have informed the doctor of her condition, perhaps left notes telling her where the next metered dose was hidden, like chocolate eggs in an Easter round up. My guilt prevents all this. They'll find her when it's far too late. It's too late already. I cannot love, though I can grieve; except for some residue of affection brought about by fate or chance, some fortune sweeping into sympathy or laughter, I'm totally impassive. I wear the pathetic cardigan she's knitted for me; too small, it feels like a singlet or waistcoat. I shiver on the platform in the drizzle looking like a grass seed on the wind, smell coal-smoke drifting like a fart across the sordid valley; no, there is nothing in the future, but I won't die yet. Sustained by anger, I suppose. The sheer unwillingness to pour wax over a dead life, refusing to reap joy from straining an artifice.

Take that last party with Ainslie. Such a thing difficult to imagine now ... a last supper intended for the immortality of sentiment or the ridding of old friends. She invited past lovers to her new penthouse, and we all began soberly enough, drinking, dividing into classes, angling for laughter with threadbare wit, worms of anxiety in the gut. It was a tense evening, an electrical storm theatrically grazing the banks of the Thames and diplomacy was sovereign for the first half-hour. Then things got complicated and people started arguing, or going into corners, as I did with Janice, who wanted so much to tell me of her life with her sixty-five-year-old artist, Randy something or other, an American, who lost it at fifty and has been painting flaccidly ever since. I mean, what the hell, Janice said, one thing I taught myself ... life never gives you much, but the best thing you can do for someone else is to nurture their fantasy. I admired Janice for her insight. Then Ainslie came by and I thought yes, I was doing that to her, nurturing a fantasy which she enjoyed, when suddenly a remarkable thing happened, for Janice began to expose one, then the other, of her perfumed charms to me, so marvellous, these undressings of the psyche and in less than no time Ainslie and Janice began a ritual coupling, almost a monastic discipline of protracted kissing and baring and the others were all so embarrassed, tethered in the tensions of their own jealousies and loyalties and teasings (yes, Janice and Ainslie now entwined like serpents), they slunk away with formal excuses, spinning in the spell of confusion. I watched it, excluded until the end when Ainslie turned and said to me, you really ought to get out of Hammersmith.

Life then was full of such vicariousness, but I'd learned the art of dispossession and if anything was going to stand me in good stead, it was this ... the notion of wonder, perhaps of wandering, entailed the lightness of never imposing, never straining form; an old nomadic custom.

About six months later Ainslie disappeared. There was an article in a London paper, the usual Fleet Street beat-up about white slavery or something similarly predictable. But there was an advertisement which looked authentic, placed by her father, asking her to contact home from wherever she was.

I remember that just months before she'd generously offered me her apartment in Russell Square. I'd work there, usually from eight in the morning till three in the afternoon, then I'd pack what I'd written in an old briefcase and take the Tube home. The next morning I'd find the place cleaned, the waste-basket emptied and the fridge full of food and wine. My mother said I was looking well, for my cheeks were flushed and my shirts grew tight. Stromboli's been good to you, she said. But I wasn't writing well. I knew deep in my heart that Ainslie's motives were never clear; if she gave, she also took away. Her gifts obligated the recipient, and such expenditure by the wealthy was really a need to destroy, to squander, to subjugate everyone who came in contact with her. This suspicion of gifts was also a nomadic instinct. The first confirmation of it was when she bought the apartment opposite. On long, lonely afternoons I'd watch her through the spy-hole bringing back new friends, and I observed her, when I met her on the landing or in the lift, growing old, her hair at times rain-flecked, matted, her clothes more and more shabby, her eyes pouched. Her friends were always young and though she looked less and less like herself, they resembled her in the way that she was, before she let herself go ... young men and women, usually blonde, with a fey quality which may have been drug-induced. I remember the day she danced out of the lift with three or four of them, draped in a red, yellow and black sheet.

After Ainslie's disappearance, it took a long time for me to summon up the courage to visit her family home in Devon. The butler refused to admit me, thinking I was a reporter. When I stopped speaking and then shuffled around and asked if at least he could call a taxi for me because these estates were out in the middle of absolutely nowhere and I needed to get to a train station and that I'd walked the last five miles and was so tired and enraged I could and really wanted to set fire to a barn or two, he finally asked me to wait. I waited for about an hour, expecting the police to drive up; at least I'd get a ride into town.

It was always the same with me. I'd say one wrong thing and then another would follow and sooner or later

I would be in trouble. Yet the wrong moves were a genuine impatience with diplomacy and convention, and when that had me by the throat I'd get on my bicycle and turn and turn about, looking for trouble, for motion invested itself in me then and I became the emissary of destruction. It was up to me to make the correction, find the drift, the current of change, to remedy that condition. But all too often I grew impatient, as I was now, having come down to Devon wanting to find out anything at all about Ainslie's disappearance, still feeling a duty there, a responsibility for those moments of tender honesty we once shared, when in the very act she would tell me how deep I had gone, so deep as to have touched the hand of the Holy Ghost. Yet even then, with that tremulous and sacred promise, there had been no children, but another counterfeit of life ... a lie, a joke once again, a handshake with metaphysics when biologically there had only been a series of purposefully sabotaged connections. I went down because she had once been family, not because of tutored sophistication or unquenched prurience.

There was also another thing.

Those letters from Emma. A month or so before, I had been receiving them from a place called Smithton in Tasmania. They were full of admiration at first, but she soon began to admonish me for not taking action against injustice. A coward at the best of times, I could nevertheless be roused. After a few bottles, a vigilante against self-righteousness. Masquerading as myself, I had made the mistake of assuming my readers would at least subscribe to one tiny part of the idea that work and author were separate. Yet now I discovered that I'd been pushed back to a literalness, to what Voltaire meant when he wrote: *I raise the quill, therefore I am responsible.*

The challenge disturbed me. I wrote back explaining that I would never do the things I wrote about, but I certainly did contemplate them. Was I therefore guilty?

Emma struck at the very paradox of my existence. In denouncing fraudulence, how could I not act? She began to demand, in a more strident tone, that I do the same for her ... make a double entry in the accounts, balance the books. I had a suspicion that this was Ainslie in disguise.

I pored over an atlas. I had written, very fleetingly, since I had never been there, about Tasmania (I don't believe I even mentioned the name) in one of my earlier novels. I put all this down to coincidence and monomania. Other writers I spoke to said that they received hundreds of such fan letters. Lucky them. Nevertheless, something nagged at me and so I made the long journey down to Devon.

At about noon Ainslie's father appeared, stomping down the grand staircase dressed for golf in checked plus fours, waistcoat and tie under his tweeds and wearing a cap with a sort of bunny's tail on the top.

Hello, boy, he said. One of Ainslie's friends, are we?

I knew he wouldn't recognise me ... he was drunk at the wedding and had never seen us since, but I took exception to his disregard for my age.

I'm her ex, I said.

He did not miss a beat but summoned up two gins, blustering with his silver hair among the golf bags in the corner, his face ruddy with the morning's snorts. There was a frozen sea between us, but we were joined by the need for commerce.

I have a proposition for you, he grunted.

He asked if I played golf. I answered in the negative, courtesy preventing me from disclosing contempt for that loathsome and parvenu game.

Never mind, old boy. It's like smacking a delicious bottom till you get to the green and then putting the ball into a hairy hole. The fewer strokes the better. It's all masochism, what?

It must have been impotence or frigidity that I tried to imagine, so presently I thought of Freud, then of Ainslie.

Don't know, old boy, her father said, when I asked about his daughter. Goes off, you know, on jaunts, sometimes for years at a time. You know anything about her politics?

No.

Me neither. But ever since she was a child she exhibited a common side. Mind you, that's not always bad. In the field chaps like that often got you out of a scrape; you'd never expect it of the rank and file.

He handed me a package. Well, you're a smart chap. You need time to think over this. I'll be in touch.

Then he was gone. The butler offered to call a taxi.

A few weeks later, Byron Johnson took his mother for a holiday.

But right now he's on the train, having left her in Wales. He's on the train careening through the dark towards London, looking at his watch, watching lorries bogged in snowdrifts on the motorways, thinking of his mother asleep before the coal fire when he'd kissed her cold cheek farewell. The firelight of reflection; all else a frozen sea.

At Waterloo station, unnerved by the human wave sweeping past, he decided against going to the publisher's party. They could launch the book without him, and then it'll be something of a five-minute wake before they'd drink and be relieved he wasn't there.

He flipped through some credit cards, his only links with Ainslie, and watched the departure boards, the flipping signs as he flipped his plastic cards, attempting a docking with a missing woman in a deep-blue night, the gulf between them a matter of degrees before miscalculation and eternity ... flip-click, the boat train to Paris ... flip-click, Zeebruge ... flip-click, Brussels. Outer space. He was hypnotised by the names of his father's war pressing down upon him, the collective weight of corpses.

Ypres. No cry of joy there. The familiar horrors descend periodically and I feel the approach of a fit. Have to tread carefully along a straight line, tell the story, no deviations; one inch out here and there and the seizure would take ... an electrical storm in the brain, a permanent digression, and wham! A smell of sulphur.

Moments like these I used to go in search of a health club. I remember that there were none in Ypres. Don't know how it came about really, the first time I visited in my youth, one of those dirty weekends when some of us decided to spend a few quid on Parisiennes and I decided I had heard a higher calling, all the more fool me, and shipped to Belgium instead with my bicycle. I needed to sweat, to lift heavy weights, grind the muscles, form scar tissue, exorcise the demon. I needed to prepare my body, knew that one day I would need to call on it, would need it to define my being, correct and re-shape time. One day I would find myself in penal servitude. May as well have been ready.

Not a single gymnasium in Ypres. Just when I was beginning to feel doomed, I found a school, and as it was a weekend, it happened to be empty. The cleaning woman (wearing a long blue apron, frumpy dress hitched around her thick calves which were covered, I could see, with a dubious rash) thought I was staff, and smiled and said, Yes, of course I could use the weights and the bars and the vaulting horse, and would I like a coffee before I began? I declined and she watched me through my paces, lasciviously, I thought, until I saw this inane smile on her face, her eyes staring at the roof, and then I realised she was partially blind and was enjoying the sounds I made, the wheezes and grunts and the heavy breathing and then presently she started making them too, copying me as she mopped and brushed and waxed the wooden boards, and in this duet of discipline, in this fugal floor exercise, in this counterpoint of counterweights we were united by a subtle mockery of our respective missions: work made you free.

It had more irony to come. But there you are: I had never been a self-deprecating liberal limited by short-sightedness. Those of us who took steps for freedom were stolid working men. She would have seen everything in her youth: this school used as a medical station for mutilated men; in the distance the crump of shells and the smell of mustard gas, the amputated arms and legs she tossed into barrels and wheeled the trolleys to the gaping ditch.

I cycled through the fields of Flanders then and took my little map of where the great battles had taken place, finding myself suddenly in a pasture with black-faced sheep grazing. I was staring at a sign which said: *Plaine d'Amour* and the thought of the thousands of bodies lying beneath suddenly burst my eardrums, sounds of them crawling through the earthworks and calling to me, their mouths filled with worms and water and mud, their shouts forming exploding shells, great starbursts of fire and dirt.

I cycled at full tilt, the monstrous sounds of Armentières, Messines, Wytschaete, Hollebeke, Gheluwelt, Zonnebeke, Passchendaele and Poelcappelle issuing from my throat and, finally, at the cemetery in Hooge I could no more and fell to the ground and I heard the gurgle and slump of a million bodies being sucked into the bowels of Flanders, not one corner of a foreign field exempt from putrid flesh oozing through the soil, oh, the ancestral stench of it, when all of a sudden I noticed someone was standing quite near, asking if I was all right ... a girl with a flower in her hand and a whimsical smile on her lips, and I greeted her, she who was pale and thin ... of such scenes are novels made ... but no, truth and more truth it had embarrassment and fear and suspicion and all the attendant horrors of real meetings.

For a brief moment I relished her foreignness but then realised, quite quickly I thought, how I might have presented, you know, the froth around my mouth not quite apparent as I was lying at an angle and was able to use my shoulder to conceal it and the rictus of my jaw which once had charm, a slight sardonic drift, proleptic and convenient, in the event of any occasion which could profitably be turned into irony ... the turn cost me, I can tell you, but I summoned immense courage and extended my humanity, a poor prosthetic French and lo! exclamation being the better part of dullness: when attempting to be interesting, always express surprise ... lo! she turned out to be French and not Belgian, though with these language struggles of theirs you never know how offensive you can be.

She wore a light dress of purple silk and though the weather was leavening ... other things too, were rising to the surface ... and though it was Easter or Pâques, which is really Passover, she did not remind me of a covered statue like those shrouded eminences I'd found in cathedrals, but her dress caught the wind and passed over her body in waves, and as it was misty she shivered beside me as I gave her a lift back to Ypres on my solid black bicycle, which was made in Shanghai and which sustained not the slightest dent or warp when I landed so heavily on the battlefield.

We had coffee by a cathedral, possibly rebuilt, possibly new in cathedral terms, totally inauthentic, a simulacrum of the original which was erected in the thirteenth century. It was planned like a cross and terminated in a semicircular choir, the central portal surrounded by a polygonal rose-window, and above, a high gable enclosed by turrets, a circulating gallery forming a passageway right around the building. All gone now, that which projected the light of the Supreme Architect who is now dead pounded into dust and mud by 16½ inch guns, seared with asphyxiating gas and laced with enfilading fire. Targeted finally, the mean point of impact discovered, there was the final destruction of time, the killing of the Mother. Guilt.

I was always guilty leaving my mother, guilty of writing because she hated it, guilty of social mobility ... and that destruction of all the Notre-Dames relieved me of it. It wasn't hatred, but relief from the burden of her centralisation, from the melancholy of her prison, from the penury of her time ... relief from the Mother that was Britain.

I told the girl all this in a French full of cavities as we talked over our café lacuna ... yes, bottomless cups, cratered cakes, crumbling lace, everything reminded one of bombs ... she of her limited life and I of my even more limited one ... and I found that she was a student at the university, but she lived with a family which wasn't her own because it was common to be boarded out when one was a student, and in a stammering and stuttering we turned the topics this way and that in our hands and wondered about them, when presently it began to drizzle and grow cold, so we walked about a bit and visited the cathedral.

We stood before a statue of the Virgin with Child and a warm feeling came over me, that same warm feeling they told us at school would come over us, not when we peed in our beds but when we thought we had a calling to the faith, which was not to be mistaken for a true calling; and all this gave me cause to reflect that religion was relief, a deliverance from what we cannot understand, and as we stood there, before the Virgin with Child, an old man, possibly a veteran of that war to end all wars, suddenly shouted, screamed, PUTAIN! PUTAIN!, his eyes fixed on the statue, so I didn't know whether he meant the girl beside me or the Virgin and I didn't know whether to take offence and boot him up the behind, crutches and all, or to have a philosophical discussion about hell. Then presently he walked away, spitting on the floor, yes, as he turned, spat on the marbled floor, his eyes glazing over us, his spittle frothing as I ushered the girl out, her face marmoreal as if this happened regularly, and we walked the streets and I was feeling strange, not knowing what was blasphemy and what wasn't, and was resolved, for one moment, to witness just once in my life a cathedral destroyed again.

We talked soon enough and grew repetitious, but repetition forced some friction upon our bodies and we were afire before too long and we rode to a wood she knew which was not far away, she on the crossbar, sitting sideways on my jacket, which kept rubbing against the front wheel, developing a sizeable hole, my one and only jacket acting as a mudflap, then in the wood another chivalrous stupidity, I laid it on a dry spot and discovered, too late, sheep pellets squashed into the lining, the dry spot a little raised where I made a bed with my jacket as we began proceedings, during which she appeared extremely sad, but it was a casual sadness, or perhaps an indifference, no puffing and preening for effect; so I dared and didn't dare, uncertain of her experience and knowing mine was of a standard practice, until finally she inserted me and it wasn't until a long time after that I noticed there were tears on her cheeks, warm then cold, and I, being naïve, asked her if it was that bad but she shook her head and said that for a very long time she had been unable to cry.

Well, I didn't know what to make of this, causing a girl to cry, for it wasn't, as far as I understood, a case of virginity lost, so I folded my jacket, pretended to be busy in order to give myself time to think, for at seventeen these things were a little deep for me, when she suddenly got up, smoothed her purple dress, took me by the hand and told me we'd been lying atop a burial site. Yes, *Pleine d'amour,* they simply threw the bodies into holes and covered them over, and I was a little annoyed with her then, and shouted: Why didn't you say something? And then I said it was indulgence of the worst kind, that callous nostalgia and pointless blasphemy, in the same way as before that war's end they were already producing postcards of the battlefields, on the verso of which the army circled whatever was appropriate:

> *Your husband/father/son/brother was:*
> a) killed
> b) missing in action
> *has sustained*
> c) serious injuries
> d) slight injuries
> e) a wound
> f) a mental condition

In 1919 the Michelin tyre company ran tours. In wicker baskets strapped on the top of the buses were champagne bottles wrapped in wet towels. All over the muddy countryside women were looking for their missing husbands. They ran to the buses, thinking the army had returned them.

Indulgent? Crying? The girl looked at me with eyes ablaze. Was that not what you were doing when you met me?

No, I said. They were tears of rage, rage against all

motherlands who sent us out to asylums, morgues, to these fields of evil. It was necessary loss, this expenditure of the common soldier. I raved and ranted, said those vile tears of mine never broke but ran deeply in unknown caverns, repositories for all the ritual evils for which families stand: the nobility of destruction. One should deserve it.

This was childish and melodramatic stuff. In the end she shook her head gravely and her face hardened. She did this, she said, to pay for her board ... no, not what we had just done, but she took touring parties to the great battlefields and sometimes she planted things, a bullet here and there, a canteen, a rusted bayonet. Tourists paid handsomely. But what we had just done, she said ... the significance of what we had just done you will never understand. Then she got on my bike and rode away and I never saw her again and felt dumb and angry because I had to walk ten miles back.

That was something from my past. I carry the incident around like a worry bead and I feel a great weight pressing down ... the discomfiture of a pea under twenty mattresses. I take the Tube for Heathrow. I have a terrible fear of flying. Suppose this weight pulls me southward, down, gravity-driven, into the ocean? I have consulted doctors about this. They peer into my heart and knead their cigars. Don't grouch about it, they say. Gravity is good in the humanities business ... a sedentary life ... you can't expect anything more than haemorrhoids.

But suppose this feeling drowns me before I get the

chance to point out the man at the end of the carriage, the tall one hanging onto the safety strap with one arm, the fellow I've seen coming and going, in and out of Ainslie's apartment? He has a box slung from a harness around his shoulder; a box wrapped in a cloth of red, black and yellow colours. I'm sure it's the same fellow ... a one-armed man. I move forward, but the train stops and he, wearing a black leather jacket and corduroy trousers, he with a day's growth of beard on a chiselled face, temple veins throbbing energetically beneath a mop of straw-coloured hair, disappears into the crowd of black-jacketed Bovver Boys hanging around the escalator. I follow but there are more of them upstairs, smoking beneath the No Smoking sign, and I feel vaguely foolish and insane, following strangers who may or may not be my ex-wife's lovers (yes, love is war: acquisition and propriety), and soon I was seeing him everywhere, a football fan with a flag under his arm, moving through the crowds on a mission for club and country.

1801. Thomas McGann. Or McGahern. Or McGahan. Difficult to know how to pronounce it, especially round about the turn of the nineteenth century. *McGunn, o'course.* Four feet nine inches, fair complexion, straw coloured hair, aged fifteen. Two years in Middlesex gaol. Transported 1799. Eight years for indecent exposure during Royal procession. Bared his bum at mad George as the carriage clattered past. But the thing about McGann ... he had this other side: self-promotion. *Aye, let me tell you 'bout meself. If you please.* The authorities took notice. Polite but not wheedling. He served five years in Port Jackson, New South Wales, and was freed by servitude when he was indentured to a settler family in the Hawkesbury district.

Borin'. Wha' d'you do ten thousand miles from home and no hope of ever returnin'? You watch the crows fly one way in the mornin' and then you watch them fly t'other in the evenin'.

Thus began a dull life, sweltering in the summers tending tomatoes and cabbages, planting barley and turnip, half of which was eaten by insects, carrying water from the river in wine barrels, walking the vegetable rows in moronic suckling; irrigating, pruning, slapping at flies and mosquitoes in the sticky air of the plains. Boring.

Mechanically, McGann daydreamed. His Irish and Scots ancestry had carefully bred obedience and anarchy. *Always had a greater purpose. Inserted it when they drew breath.* But this multiculturalism, this sense of not belonging, gave him an advantage: in a new country the future was his. *Thought a lot 'bout Bonaparte. My hero, sorta.* He was not concerned with what had already occurred. He wasn't interested in revenge, or how it would otherwise have been, his life in Liverpool, his mother's face appearing in the crowd, jeering, swatting at his head when she became desperate and drunk, but nowhere to be seen when the soldiers appeared and led him away. *'Ere we go, 'ere we go, 'ere we go!*

On Sundays, on the Hawkesbury, the Bosanquets forced him to church, where he sat in a pew trying not to breathe and thus, without breathing, willed the service and the pastor's platitudinous droning to end, to suffocate, to explode. *Oooh. Ahhh.* He thought he could faint to shorten the process. But one thing prevented it. Mrs Bosanquet, for some strange reason, left her knickers in the woodshed. It happened more than once and he didn't think fit to mention them, giving himself to understand that it was an act of charity. She had seen the holes in his clothes. She had stressed cleanliness. But the knickers ... Perhaps she was embarrassed. He wore them under his trousers. He couldn't faint. What grew light on top ... his head faded into balloons ... grew heavy beneath. Mrs Bosanquet's underpants excited him, her unmentionables next to his skin. He didn't have to make any effort not to melt into air. Yet his desires confronted emptiness and this thorn kept reality close, for he was unable to explain to himself how an older woman like her could have all the manipulative skills of a passionate lover and yet dole out the dangerous supplement of a never-to-be-consummated flirtation. She treated him like a child. *They was alway doin' that. I said I was grown up an' all, but it was the goodness what was killing me.*

McGann studied the back of Mrs Bosanquet's head. A pale neck, hair swept up to fall in ringlets, dark roots beneath. She had large, watery blue eyes, and fainted easily when the weather changed. On humid afternoons when McGann would be kneading her likeness from clay along the riverbank, in the late afternoon just before the predictable storm arrived, Mrs Bosanquet would faint on the verandah, her fan fluttering at her breast. The servants would loosen her collar. Sometimes she fainted in church and he would glimpse a lace bodice, but he was never close enough or alone so that he could do the loosening himself. *Want to know what love is? It's somethin' you feel what the upper classes alone can say. God, my heart broke! Do we love differently?*

Mr Bosanquet puffed and groaned and the pew creaked when he shifted. He smelled of worsted and tobacco and moved slowly, with the meticulous dullness of colonial commerce in his head. He was respected as a man who knew sheep and cattle, dung sprouting with straw stuck between the heel and sole of his boot. McGann could not have imagined a worse existence. As a convict he had seen floggings and hangings and yes, had developed the best motivation for staying alive:

resentment. *Oh, aye. Excitin' to see a man hanged. It brought you the rage, see?*

Something of this sort had already taken place on board ship from England. They had run into the first of several storms off the Cape, and in the ensuing mêlée he found himself in the officers' quarters when, wonder of wonders, discovered a dozen chickens kept there for higher palates. He released them through the porthole and remembered feeling immense satisfaction at their clumsy flight and futile plunges into the mighty ocean. One, however, drew altitude in manic indirection, withstood the eager reaches of spray and driving rain and headed fortuitously toward land beyond. He took this as a sign of his own manumission. Then, nearing Sydney, he contracted malaria and spent months in solitary, his face swollen, shivering in night-sweats. Given up for dead he was freed for a time, lying unnoticed in a puddle by the Quay until a fellow inmate dragged him up, forcing him to sip a concoction a Chinaman had recommended: hairless, new-born rats marinated in rum. *'Twasn't a matter o' taste. You swallowed without chewin.* He recovered. A magistrate found reason to return him to chains. He was patient and earned release again.

But the rustic piety and continuous homily at the Bosanquets had no concern for the diseased reality of life, at least not with this one. That is, if it weren't for Mrs Bosanquet. Who had taught him to read. Her breath sweet on his neck as she pushed her finger haltingly over the words; ever onward. She taught him Latin. He memorised without effort: amo, amas, amat.

He breathed in.

Terra australis: an open-air prison, he was thinking, as she read to him about Napoleon's exploits.

He breathed out. A strand of Mrs Bosanquet's hair lifted and she half turned. He saw her glorious ear. But he had not the words which she would want to hear.

On Sundays he was not to work, so he lingered near the house after church and did carvings. Out of selected boxwood, he made figurines so fine he could have whittled a new life for himself, but he showed them to nobody and thought badly of his skill. He considered himself a simpleton and these were simple pastimes.

He was told repeatedly that religion and work were the important things and that he was someone who should never aspire beyond his station. So he was more than a little aghast when religion continually brought him to the back pew behind Mrs Bosanquet's neck, and religion led him to examine her body with impunity and to unclothe her and to touch her. *Never, never, never.* For the boredom of religion had given him the power of extreme imagination, to the point at which, coupled with his short and dramatic life, he was unable to manage reality without convincing himself of some illusory purpose. It was warped; it was fundamental and exciting ... really of no relevance in the mounting of Mrs Bosanquet, in the kissing of her neck while frothing in ecstasy, in the fondling of her breasts, in the insertion of himself with wild transgression ... of no relevance at all when everything was imagined and no insight revealed itself, no issue of fact save the pounding insistence in his trousers, the pressure there when he decided, one Sunday afternoon, to call on her with an armful of figurines ... his best work … little dancing faeries, winged ballerinas, all etched with fine scales of ringleted hair he had once glimpsed in a painting. *Never.*

He tapped at the kitchen window and a maid appeared, shooing him away with her hands. He asked for the mistress. She wasn't in. The maid had seen her take the sulky towards the river, perhaps to meet her husband on the road from town. Mr Bosanquet would stop at the hotel of course, if the river flooded. The hotel had markings on the wall near the steps: the height of flood-water cut into the stone. The marks were very high. Sometimes Mr Bosanquet would not be home for days.

He walked back by the woodshed and saw the sulky, the horse tethered by the willows, and with heart beating irregularly stole up to a crack in the bark wall and saw Mrs Bosanquet jigging up and down, performing a kind of dance, though she was on her knees and unclothed, and he watched with fascination how one of her breasts was smaller than the other and how she was red in the face and perspiring, her eyes closed, then half-closed, and she moved her head from side to side as one who was taken with the falling sickness, and then rougher arms came up to steady her, holding her hips, and he saw the pastor lying on a horse-rug beneath her, his arms falling back as though he were struggling in water and about to drown. *Imagination. Reality. I care not which.*

McGann put his nose to the gap. Ironbark. River loam. Perfume. Semen. This was the pious otherworld. Cicadas intensified their scraping until their drumming came in regular rhythms of deafening noise which reflected his isolation. He tore at strands of his hair. His jealousy was immense, a sweet, sexual pain held in infinite contradiction. And then the little chirring sounds the pastor was making broke through, Mrs Bosanquet's gasps punctuating them.

Cheated of his manhood, he turned, came to a kind of crossing, a muddied corduroy of logs, and he sat and placed his feet in the warm liquid and watched insects swim and dart away. He squashed a few. The black mud changed and reformed in fluid consistency. He looked at the bubbles and suddenly knew, though he had scarcely the words to convey the insight, knew that he would have to weave his own image in the darkness of this world. Fatherless, motherless, to forever perform a corrective to the corrections of authority. *Which was tryin' always to silence those who really needed to speak.*

He picked up an axe. Hesitated. Chaos was his. It would come as suddenly and as naturally as a baby's first gasp of air. A slap and then the fury, the splintering bone and gushing blood, the cries and gurgles of this furious world. He would see them begging, pleading, on their knees in the same way as they took their pleasure. The crunch of skull beneath. Fleeting life.

But for now it was enough to have seen it, to have had the powerful desire to take it away. He shouldered the axe and followed the river. At a bend he cast his figurines into the water and watched them float off. He walked until he reached the sea, contemplated there awhile, his finger in his nose ... about the peace of islands and the natural order; the domain of love about which he had heard; maidens with flowers in their hair ... his fancy peppered with the grapeshot of the Napoleonic enterprise, missions of conquest and skilful dominion, visions to weave his own future outside the oppressive presence of an authorial hand.

They were building ships at the mouth of the river. He managed to become a swab on one that looked likely to sink on its maiden voyage.

From the log of the *Nora,* a brig commanded by Capt. O. Pennington-James:

> McGann deserted his first ship in Cloudy Bay, New Zealand. They all had the feckin' desire to do that: frisk with native women and produce a new patriarchy, monarchy, whatever, of ministering maidens ... but they usually got eaten or thrown off clifftops or burned ceremonially. But by golly, I give it to this McGann. He must have had the good fortune or manner to ingratiate himself, for he lived for some time with a bevy of Maori women.
>
> If it can be believed, McGann told us how on an East Coast trek one summer ... they did these treks quite regular ... they all slid down a glacier in a Kauriwood canoe, attacked periodically by a giant, flightless bird ... well, every mariner turned marooner came up with such stories to hide failure. McGann was either a consummate liar or a feckin' simpleton and, I think, expected good hazing from all.
>
> But then there was the time when we encountered war canoes off the Bay of Islands and why, McGann spoke so fluently and convincingly in

> their tongue (theirs were stuck out to horrify us, fluttering purple athwart their lips) that soon the natives were pressing upon us more fruit and potatoes than we could have possibly stowed. We were in such calm we anchored awhile and the men spent the following week lazing, pulling at the scuttlebutt and sitting 'round the longboat until they had to be humbugged into mending the rigging.

Spouter off larboard!

Pennington-James lays aside his quill and goes on deck with the brass speaking trumpet. Cavalho, the Portuguese third mate, points. Eighty yards off the prow a black whale surfaces, blows, swings playfully sideways to eye them off, dives and circles back. Pennington-James yells to the helmsman to keep the ship on course, driving the whale leeward to shallower water. Pretty soon they see two others, then a pod of five or six, altogether about 400 to 500 barrels, Pennington-James calculates, for this is his specialty, the quickness of mind when it comes to figures, let's see, at £13 per ton, he was looking at £2000 right there, these the Right whales, he muses, his mind already computing the £200 he would earn for this trip.

Lower the boats!

The men don't need to be told. McGann's chocked the steering oar when they swing the boats out, the davits groaning, like riding a horse now, bending his knees as he releases the rope, waiting for the dip of waves to drop the whaleboat in, whipping away the wooden pulley yelling Heads! a split second too late as it swings back towards the ship, hoping to catch a swab a good one on the head, but there are no takers and they are used to this and they duck and are soon pulling steadily towards the rocky shore and the emerald furrow of dangerous water, pulling hard because the tide is giving them no chance for error as they feel the pull of the swell and the black water heaves and suddenly they're closing on a curious whale and Cavalho's stuck it, but not too well for the iron draws, Cavalho pulling in, his hands blood-crusted, the whale's eye turning cloudy in pain, now trying to scythe them with its flukes. They strike again and this time the black fish sounds, the rope whipping and whirring from the tubs, smoking the blocks, and when the beast glides up McGann deftly plunges a lance into its heart and it blows a terrible trumpet of blood and tissue into the boat, everything smeared now, the men in a frenzy, making fast an anchor by drilling through its flukes and he, fixing a rod into its back, runs up a white whiff.

Aye, these black fish have no real will to fight, he says as the sun peeps out, lighting up the water. Eeee. Eeee. They say they have a song, chirruping underwater to each other. Poor barnacled flanks which will become bubble and squeak and the scented oil of night providing for our education, weak eyes and the attrition of desire.

Before too long he sights three others and they gain on them and separate them, harpooning two, but the third escapes with two hundred yards of line in its back, trailing a red wake in the aquamarine.

By dusk a nauseous wind has risen and when Pennington-James heaves the ship to and lowers sail, he counts twenty-two carcases, some anchored, some running towards the shoal water. He orders McGann to bring two alongside. When the boats are up they begin the cutting in, wasting no time while the weather is calm, standing on stages lowered from davits, wielding bounding knives, swaying and stripping, their backs lit by the try-pot fires roaring beneath the cauldrons, strips of winched blubber sliding sticky with blood back along the deck, innards oozing and sucking at their feet. Black smoke, blackened men, rancid air, a ship afire. The natives on shore watch in fascination, marvelling at this industry of devils.

By morning the wind has intensified. There is nothing to be done and the ship is beginning to drag its anchor. After a while they hoist the sails and depart, leaving twenty whale carcases buffeting the boulders, pieces of blubber floating in red froth, the natives poking at them, tasting bits, watching the rest roll into inlets and coves, setting up an almighty stink.

The ship made sail in the firming wind and ploughed northward. In the lazaret three captured women lay, exhausted, turning in pools of vomit, faecal matter and bilge water, wretched from the tossing, bucking and swaying. McGann went down there, the air fouled with sickly blubber and blood. He brought salted pork and a slops bucket and cleaned them, gently rubbing their skin with gin and water, their teeth chattering. There now. They trembled. There now. They ate for the first time, chewing slowly. The one he had designated was his, the one he loved most, the one called WORÉ.MER.NER., smiled at him.

At noon, Pennington-James called McGann to his cabin.

I've decided to lay over a bit, he said. See what we can pick up. I'm getting the hang of this here whaling.

Sealing's the thing, Sir. We're too small for whales.

Hmmm. But you see, McGann, there's nothing to sealing. If you think that small you'll end up scooping scampi. I know the *Nora's* only a brig, but if you get the men down below with the oakum ... plug all the beams with tar, we'll do this aright. Square her up, McGann.

Pennington-James didn't tell McGann that he thought whaling was more dramatic, that he needed whaling in order to write his private log. Pennington-James didn't mention the cart he was putting before the horse, the book before real life, writing before whaling. Pennington-James wanted to compose the definitive whaling novel while nibbling on crayfish and sipping a crisp semillon. He wanted to put down the greatest fish story of them all, just when a youngster by the name of Melville slipped out of Albany Classical School to begin a life at sea.

I'll make the decisions about this ship, he continued, avoiding McGann's eye, taking off his spectacles for that purpose. You'll see by and by what's best for us.

Sperm McGann didn't see at all. Down below in his hammock he plied pieces of old hemp. Then he went down into the lazaret and flicked it at the legs of the women. They thought it was a game and giggled at first, but when it didn't stop, suffered it noiselessly.

Gravity drew me down. The gravity of letters. I knew from experience what dependency could lead to. Emma's grief would be great if she met me, just think of it, an oik from Hammersmith (Hammersmith, *Thames-side inner borough; industl., residtl., elec. and car accessories, synthetic rubber*), what do I know of psychological dependency? What do I know of the healing process? Better remain silent, rear my ugly head at the right moment and not put pen to paper for the purposes of communication. Better the bearer of delicacy: observe, repine, empathise from a great distance, than to fester a wind-swept isle with hotfooted assuagement from the other side of the colonial Styx.

Yet to stem the hurt now, was that not insurance for a happy meeting? A prolepsis, no less, to tell her: Fear not, I'm coming to you, and thus, having arrived, not fear the unknown? And further: Together we will discover what you cannot say. And each time I will grow dizzy and we will draw closer. A déjà vu is better than an imprévu, I say.

But then a potential suicide and a repressed schizophrenic can be a volatile mix. Witness her latest missive:

some ancestral memory of whaling; natives amidships in the forbearing line; sentences cut into chaotic boroughs of tribal dialects, somewhat like Fulham. A jigsaw. A problematic.

I wasn't Freud. I tried to reason it out. Tell a story with a point to it, and unlike Kafka, try to sell books. Maybe, against my better judgment (and how that has failed me over the years!) I will send her my most innovative book, printed on loose-leaf and bound in a ring folder (much to the annoyance of my publisher ... you can see him drinking to my demise which he regards as much as his own), so the reader could read just the plot if fancy overtook him/her; and in the subtle shifting of identity, gender, class, age, whatever was unleaving from the constriction of rings, retire to the real chaos of our imaginations.

Strangely enough, Emma's letters gave me life. The startled energy of the mad and, thanks to British Post, teasingly delayed in Dickensian instalments. I harboured suspicions, of course, that they were Ainslie's. Some bizarre torture she had invented to keep me interested. One day she will come back to me like a Capistrano swallow. Fallacious as that may be, I gave myself credit for vanity. My self-confidence rarely peeps.

But then you couldn't blame me, for suddenly in the mail came five credit cards, shinily embossed with my name, each debited to her account, A. Cracklewood, upon checking. I wasn't a bank Johnny once for nothing. There were conditions. I had one expense for each, one wish limited to £1000. In effect, £5000 to pursue a whim. It was the normal patron's grant, generous, over-generous, though I didn't raise a finger to my flat cap; no Ma'am. Ainslie had taught me well. There was always the greater obligation of a return gift which bound us more closely than a marriage, which tribal people knew, trying to outdo each other in gifts until the ultimate destitution of one or the other. We the civilised, call it consumption ... the rich give in order to decree debt, to accrue interest. Nothing so refined as mere obligation.

Consumption. I have a pain in my chest. There, just to the side. Sometimes it stretches into my back and it becomes painful to breathe. I take shallow breaths, feel faint, fall. The doctors in London said it wasn't consumption; something pleural nevertheless, mounting up. Perhaps an intercostal virus. Not wanting to live, I let myself be drawn.

Gravity. Drawing me down. From the plane I could see a kind of hole in the sky; a glaring, icy sun.

Tasmania.

Madness in its name.

In London, when I saw a crowd, I joined it. When they threw bricks through train windows I clapped. When I heard a band or chanting Hare Krishnas or even the toneless singing of shameless or desperate buskers, I stamped my foot in time, shook, danced, until the police moved me on. To be connected to the stream of life; otherwise to melt, to unload the till, reveal the drift I carry with me: deliquescent clocks, thawed stress, rage enough to kill. The other things formed a solidity, kept me in touch with being. Yes, to sling a rope across, that was my mission; to walk myself over the liquid abyss. Then over the hill. No, they didn't include me in *The Best Of British Novelists.* If you look at their photos they're all so pretty and young. Mere babes.

In Hobart I walked the other way. Kept back even from those milling about for luggage in the rain. I covered my ears, closed my eyes. There were no crowds, bands or slogans. So close now, I would receive no more letters. I went straight to the Sheraton, booked in, cocooned myself in glass and kept my drift intact. It was a dangerous weight and I knew it.

Registration.
Name: Byron Shelley Johnson.
Origin: Hammersmith, London, England.
Card: AmEx. Slightly bent.
Description: Dark. Seemly through a glass. Probably of melancholic disposition until there's drink or women. Suspiciously overweight. Something pressing him down, the duty to be jovial.

I know. First thing I did was to go to the health club. Not to exercise, but to stand on the scales. I thought the plane trip, a sedentary marathon, would have trimmed off some poundage through nervous exhaustion, fear of flying, the terror of inane conversations. I thought I was free, rolling plugs of Ohropax into my ears, but heard the caterwauling of children and the commotion and the stupid excitement of travellers. I heard the dull pulse of a tired erection in my temple, watching the hostess strap herself into her seat. Mea culpa. I prayed for reprieve.

I've gained five pounds. I went to the sauna. A woman lying on a bench took one look at me and left. After three minutes the heat became too much. Somebody vomited in the shower. Back in my room I finished off the beers from the fridge, watched the day come to its end in cold drizzle slanting over the docks, the Derwent calm and black and the brooding sky hanging low. Hobart was a picturesque town. Hard to imagine how once it reeked with *huile de baleine,* the nauseating cologne of blubber trying out the noses of the foreshores. Took the place of homesickness, I suppose, replaced forever the scent of the Thames.

I didn't want to drink, but kept drinking. I unpacked my camera and sat by the huge window taking close-ups of boats for over an hour and then upon further focussing, suddenly discovered the glint of something strange. Screwed on my telescopic lens then and found someone else, I could see him quite clearly, backing away, possibly with a night scope directed at my window from the harbourmaster's tower. I quickly drew the curtains.

There are those who yearn for death but remain completely unconvinced by it. They carry the shadow, but mercifully the simulacrum doesn't smell: no seasoned corpses, fishy blood, the acrid tar of human suffering. But there is another kind whose fear of death is so great that they act impulsively. Get it over with silently. To be silent, and thus to pass the baton on. There's the rub. You need a clear mind. So this chafing passed soon enough. The alternative, folly, wasn't apparent at first. The blending into glass and carpet, into elevators and armchairs, the gourmet consumption and the long lug of afternoon-chasing, the slow-paced leavenings of alcohol; all this deferred the reckoning. I've come this far down. I burp for the salvation of my soul.

Nagged by privilege, my third credit card pathetically worn, I looked out at the black water and the crayfish boats moored tightly against each other. Out there, beyond the shrouded bays and granitic points, the *Nora* was nowhere in sight. Having already sailed past Shouten Island and the Freycinet Peninsula, the brig was heading for Eddystone Point and mutiny. I can smell it in the crayfish. Seasmell. Out there, an invitation to tempt the limitless. Dizzy again. Reach for the marmalade.

I am WORÉ. WORÉ *is woman.*

WORÉ *waits in the night to be given away. Waits to appease. Our men and the white men. But when they come it is not like a betrothal. Like a storm instead, while we hide behind windbreaks feeble as our hearts and they kill our brothers and bind our hands and feet, the first time in our lives we have known physical restriction. The first time, this kind of fear, not felt in nature. No, not the fear of pain or illness. A fear like a burning torch thrust into us. In the way that we killed sea elephants, putting firesticks down their throats. And then I knew why they had taken this long journey from across the water. They have come not for seals but for us, taking our skins, turning us pale when they cut into our buttocks with their sharp knives, flaying us, feeding us, pushing themselves into us, toying with us, healing us, dressing us, teaching us, selling us, beating us, forcing us to hunt, exploding us, marooning us, stroking us, plaiting our hair, feeling us, giving us firedrink, whipping us, reproducing us, painting us, making us happy, making us sad, making us something else, opening us to ourselves.*

But I am still WORÉ. *And* WORÉ *is woman, who is stronger than man.*

But for the moment WORÉ *is the beloved of McGann.*

McGann comes down into the bottom of the winged fireboat and chains me to the wall, then puts a rope around my neck and tightens it, choking me until I cannot struggle, a muttonbird caught at the mouth of a burrow and I cannot flap my wings to make the fireboat go out of my life, out of my life my heart struggles to fly, too late, too late, I have lost WORÉ, *the little girl they said I was, the beloved of McGann, for I have made him angry and cruel, but suddenly I'm gasping and the air comes into me again, and again, life returns. Suddenly McGann is touching me very softly, whimpering and moaning and falling to the ground. The fear is familiar, when he has released me. I'm still here,* WORÉ.

Breathe now. Twelve seasons old and too young yet to be killed.

The territory of the other. Not *verboten,* I assure you. I carried Emma in my heart.

I knew my destination, but for a while, Hobart was congenial. I rang my mother. She was still alive.

My legs are swelling, dear, she said. Ronnie and Millie next door've gone to the football. Having a quart of milk stout. You look after yourself and don't get home too late. Hobart ... is that up near Hertford? Don't be too long, and mind those trolley-buses when you come up the Edgeware Road.

Each day, the warm sun bursting through the ozone hole, briefly, before the clouds. Wet air infuses; wood or stone absorbs. Then the reverse. People taking off, putting on. Flesh creeps. Totally unpredictable, the weather. That was the word all the guide books used: *unpredictable.* I liked Hobart for all that. Hilly streets, flowery gardens, healthy girls on bicycles, tight rows of roses all prickly underneath, tidy generations, false pedigrees, the neat pursuit of decency, the over-reaction to it. I liked it for all that, though it could have done with whores, porno houses, all-night bars and a smattering of indifference, pretence, high-brow drugs, low-brow passions, the throb and hum of semilunacy, arrogance and violence. It used to be that way. But then of course it had the unpredictable.

Mr Johnson? Mr Byron Johnson?

I had, until now, carefully cultivated anonymity. Don't be unkind. A recluse strikes bargains with the mirror. Well, now and again the reflection of public interest. All those faces in the glass. Get a looksee. Him the fella what writes all that dirty stuff? Check the diary; look in the laundry basket. You always remember the first time. Surprise that a woman would be interested in me because I wrote. They're all romantics until they read the stuff. The reality: bump and run. She swivelling and circling, hips made for that. Sorry darlin'. Didn't give you 'arf a chance did we? Ha! Noted down. Too much mascara. Cheap, but lovely for all that. A kindness refinement takes an eternity to learn. They were all lovely women, the ones who didn't read. Important to stay in love. Not to revert to the cradle. No need for admiring eyes then.

And now it was a waitress. Attractive. Rusted pistons of the heart sucked at ancient sump oil. I was sitting by the bar nursing a cold cognac.

There's a gentleman over there would like to speak to you.

Disappointment. Apprehension. Resentment. I turned. He was standing at the desk, his back to me, reading the register. Hunched with menace, perhaps even familiar with this procedure. Pin-striped suit. As he turned, peered over a pair of half-moon glasses, his face ruddy, hair silvered, chin weak. Years of fine wines gathering around the eyes. Never did any street work. No plod then. Watched me approach, expression curious, intent. We shook hands. Hands soft.

Mr Johnson? I'm Deakin, from Immigration. (He produced a plastic card bearing a photo.) Could you spare a few minutes? Taking me by the elbow to the lounge.

I didn't care for this pushing and shoving. I took it only from women. Once, standing outside Harrods in the drizzle and searching for a health club in more salutary precincts, a policewoman nabbed me by the elbows. Pinned thus, I examined her breasts with my *latissimus dorsii*. Perfumed. Not just laundry-soaped like nuns. She had wanted to know was I not with that gang of shoplifters who'd made off with a dozen hip flasks. God, no, I said, speaking backwards to her, my mouth an inch away from hers smelling of mint, such discipline and grooming. I'm a weightlifter, not a shoplifter, ma'am. Search my hips for them if you please. She declined, released me with a warning. Difficult to feel sensual and censured at the same time. I suppose I was a big lad for sixteen.

I have to make a few inquiries about your stay in Tasmania. Your holidays. You're on holidays, aren't you? Deakin asked.

I had been told to expect this kind of thing. They kept records, computerised and beamed all over the world. Even if they didn't read my books the Secret Services focussed a telescopic eye on me. I wrote in earnest, a book before last, I think, about an explosion. Yes, once the toilets blew in the stock exchange, the City was in the shit. All those long-lunched bellies and wine-filled bladders had to be held and massaged for a block and a half until relief in a damp Tube station. Some were so frightened they did it then and there.

Yes, I'd sent a clockwork train up the sewer-line laden with gelignite. A week or two after publication it really happened. It became a celebrated copy-cat crime. It became a notorious case of fiction inspiring fact, of mistaken identity, of confusing writer and narrator, of misreading explosions, exploding misreadings, whatever. The book had something of a cult following. Universities commissioned lectures on coincidences and connections, and smaller explosions, some the size of fireworks, became regular undergraduate pranks. My publishers defended me, but the police still believed I was IRA.

Holidays from what? From terrorism?

Deakin laughed uncomfortably at this, adjusted his half-moons. He was theatrical, embarrassed, egotistical. Camped it up. Waved his fingers under his chin. Dubious, this mannerism.

Deakin: Oh no. Nothing like that. We simply need an itinerary. We, ah, we like to follow up on, ah, passport irregularities.
B.S.J.: Irregularities?
Deakin: Well, we, ah, the Department, understands that you haven't been issued one in the last five years.
B.S.J.: Is that a crime?
Deakin: Ah! It could be the result of one, yes.

(Self-satisfied; astonished; both at once. Rain outside, filtered softly through the trees.)

B.S.J.: So you think this is a forgery?

Deakin: No, but perhaps it's been altered?

B.S.J.: Hardly. The photo doesn't even look like me. I've changed in five years, a divorce thrown in. If I was a forger, I'd use a recent photo.

Deakin: Oh, no. They're very clever these days. Change their looks, their names, their skin, even their personalities. Impersonators with the psychologies to match. May I keep this for a while? *(Ample pockets. Hong Kong tailor.)*

B.S.J.: Be my guest.

Deakin: Oh, no. You're the guest. We just want to make sure you've been invited, you know, a *persona gratis.*

That last phrase was hardly necessary. Deakin was a prat. Private schoolboy regaling you with Latin from the sidelines.

Tell me, he said, lighting up a cigarette. The smoke he exhaled smelled differently to that which came from the cigarette ... presumably carrying some pulmonary component. Tell me, he said again, do you use many words in your writing?

I took this as impertinence, though for a split second Mozart came to mind, rebuked for too many notes.

Verbiage, Deakin suddenly jerked his chin towards the ceiling as though he had smelt garbage, tells you rather more about someone than they would like to admit. A slight overreaching, perhaps. Aspiration which springs from lack, need, whatever.

Like a drink? I ventured, signalling the waitress. Deakin obliged and reached into his pocket.

Which sometimes makes for a good lexicon, he smiled, slavering, though it took me a while to recognise his obsession.

Shakespeare, he intoned, used about twenty-four thousand words in his plays ... different words ... there was no evidence of alcoholism ... whereas Beckett ... He let that hang, as if to illustrate his point.

We study vocab and usage in the Department, he said.

You mean linguistics, philology, that type of thing?

Oh no. He suppressed a smile and eyed my drink. He was an alcoholic, no doubt about that; alcoholics always try to resist the first drink.

We study the language of terrorism; notes, letters, phone-calls. They are rather less minimalist than Sam Beckett. Far more interesting, of course, although Beckett was capable of a few bombs. Take *Waiting For Godot* ... that's a threat if ever there was one. No, terrorists have a vocab of about fifty to a hundred words. There's always a pattern.

Count me out then, I said.

Oh, no, Deakin sighed, saddened that I wasn't playing any longer. Not yet.

I laughed. He didn't take kindly to that.

We had a note about your arrival, he continued. What about your itinerary?

In order to avoid further word-play, psychological analysis, meticulous tedium, I foolishly took out Ainslie's map. Unfolded it and unglued the chewing gum which once held it to the wall of one of her apartments. I was hoping a picture would rescue us from another thousand words.

Let's see ... Deakin said, and pounced with a finger, his pin-striped sleeve shooting up his forearm. You've circled Cape Grim. What is it about Cape Grim which interests you? He was smiling.

Love.

Ah! Deakin wasn't smiling any longer.

I was fumbling for an explanation. I stuttered. A gulf appeared. I didn't think I was suffering another memory lapse. I knew memory lapses led to the disruption of order, when the hero makes a faux pas, takes a false step, losing his memory when he stumbles, catching his foot in a hole. Yet I needed to expose the till, to break new ground, a desire for which I had no explanation. I was afraid of that. Still, it was a foolish thing not to have remembered to bring another map ... put them off the scent ... but sentiment, you see, always leaves a trail, like perfume.

It's the clean air, I said. It's reputed to have the cleanest air in the world. Comes all the way from South America, filtered over a thousand miles of ocean without a single landfall, purified of all that garlic and *violencia* and bodies dumped from helicopters. (Yes, Cape Grim had an air-monitoring station, a sort of high-tech sniffer, a snoz keening out of the cliffs to measure purity, getting first snuffle at virgin winds.) I want to go there, I said. Clean out the bellows. I pounded my chest with my fist, coughed, felt the heaviness within.

Deakin pressed out his cigarette. Ah, he said, the poles of purity. They regulate confusion. We have a duty to distil our heritage, you know.

He grew silent and despondent and stared balefully at Ainslie's red texta mark circling that north-west corner.

Tell me, I asked. Why is it called 'Grim'?

Deakin shrugged.

Mournful history, he ruminated. Never learned much of it. All those places had grievous names.

I left him with half the bottle, saying I had to take a nap. I folded the map as he was fumbling for something in his pocket. He produced a pellet of paper and unfurled it with one hand.

You want to hear the latest, what they're writing about you in London? It's from *The Guardian*. He was seeking to detain me.

I shook my head.

He began to read anyway, his voice quavering in false tenor, like an old Ezra Pound recording:

> Johnson's work and life reveal the tragic assumption of the notion of fiction as lies. Painting himself into a corner and failing a one-to-one transfer of truth between writer and reader, he desperately tries to subvert the text.

Subversion, Byron, Deakin said. It's a dangerous game to play.

I made my escape on that warning. Before the lift doors closed, I saw him making notes with a gold fountain pen.

Ascended.

Stepped off on the fourteenth floor, went down the fire exit and took a walk by the waterfront. Had to move fast. When faced with the unpredictable, do the unexpected.

Couldn't breathe then. Felt a cold hand pressing down upon my neck.

Rage, of course, made him shallow.

Sperm McGann was standing his watch in the dark, thinking of that, transfixed by the silvery waves creasing the sea behind, the brig doing a steady four knots reaching for the Furneaux.

It was an illness, this rage, frothing his mouth and locking his jaw. They said that happened when you got bitten. There had been a dog at the Bosanquets. Mongrel on a chain which lunged at him every time he fed it. Biting the hand ...

He was at other times immensely calm. Changeable like the sea. Used to get the longboats out and tug them over the side, gently pull on his mind, ropes of thought. He wanted to know so much. Wanted to find out exactly the mechanism which drove the body. Down below, the last time off New Zealand, he'd operated on a man. The boatsteerer. Yes, the same who was flicked like a gnat off a blackfish fluke. Upside down he was, in mid-air, collarbone through the flesh, all the while Pennington-James scooting fore and aft polishing his eyeglasses, saying, Damn, the man's a goner.

Down below McGann had pushed back the bone, placed a board in front and one behind and drew them together with ropes and turnbuckles. Above the man's screaming he'd heard the crack and suddenly the air was rushing into his lungs and the poor fellow was grunting and then wheezing and then was breathing as easy as you please. But the next night the boatsteerer brought up black blood and that was when McGann cut him open, reached in with a finger and felt the penetrated lung and pushed back the splinter of bone. The man gasped, frothing with blood and died an hour later.

In there, inside the body, an immensity of thought. Someone else's work he would like to preserve, but he was hamfisted, cack-handed, his mind like granite and always within that, the fires of rage. He wanted so much to know.

He heard a movement behind.

Mishter McGann, you want for me to take your watch?

It was Cavalho, the Portuguese.

Aye, Porky. In two hours I want all the men up here. No noise.

Cavalho, one of those bull-necked seadogs who gave loyalty in return for their share of violence, pillage, rape and porter. He drank so much there was never anything in his lay after the others deducted what he owed them. McGann gave him a wooden whistle.

Three blows.

Cavalho swung himself onto the quarterdeck. Immensely powerful, he irritated all authority with his inane and provocative smile which, attended by a disconcerting astigmatism, gave him the look of a benign though unpredictable gorilla. He was smiling now, on the quarterdeck, picking something out of his ear with McGann's whistle.

A year before that smile was a comfort of sorts when Pennington-James had the brig lying off Macquarie Harbour, close-reefed as the wind whipped up and the clouds scudded across the sky and the sandbanks were coming up close, ridged with fierce spume. Suddenly they could see the wrecks rising out of the rocks so they made for the harbour, signalling in the salt haze to the semaphore station on Entrance Island, which stood guard, piteously small, next to the raging slit of Hell's Gates. Yes, Pennington-James was frightened to go in without a pilot, making whimpering sounds on deck, saying that he ought to perhaps circumnavigate Van Diemen's Land again, until better weather afforded him the grace to pass safely through. At the moment it was a maelstrom of froth and current, seven-and-a-half feet of aquamarine and then the slapping deep black water, cold and tannin-stained, of the penal harbour.

McGann drew a whaleboat, picked Cavalho and two others, and they sailed in for provisions, gaff-rigged, tide against wind, between Scylla and Charybdis, the huge rumbling seas swallowing them and for one moment they all heard the voice of God, that resonant howling heavy with judgment, an albatross gliding above. Cavalho looked up and smiled and they all thought what innocence he possessed, his wet, benighted face calming divine fury, the bird suddenly shitting in flight, gobbets of it landing in Cavalho's wall-eye as the Roaring Forties suddenly spat them into calm water. That had freed them all.

Then close-hauled, they saw a man running on the shore and as they drew in close they could see him still running, naked, genitals flailing, pallid flanks trembling, coming up against an invisible wall, raising his arms, running back, finding no escape in the dense scrub and finally squatting, exhausted, in the shallows. McGann jumped over the bow, pulled the boat in.

Take me back, the escapee rasped, hair matted, face chiselled and scarred, beard clotted with green slime, a nauseating stench from his nether regions. He was grasping a square of fish-bait.

They forced him to sit over the side, shit running down his legs, his little package neatly wrapped in kelp, and when they neared Sarah Island, saw a boatload of marines pulling out to intercept them.

The fellow spoke again before they manacled him.

I've eaten of a man, he said. Here, got some of 'im left.

He unwrapped a green piece of meat.

Should have taken him aboard, McGann was thinking, swinging in his hammock, when a shrill whistle sounded. Once. Twice. No more. Fucking Cavalho can't count. He drew a pistol from his seabag, carefully inserted a ball, seated the cap. He swung out of the hammock and went up to the Captain's cabin. The door was slightly ajar. Pennington-James was snoring. A stale waft of air emerged. A ruffle of bedclothes. A Mohair Harvard quilt.

This is it, Orville, the end of the line.

Mama, is that you?

Draw out thy hands or I'll blast thee in the bum.

This formality awoke the Captain, his mind still festooned with bedtime sea-stories.

Mercy! he cried.

He was allowed to put on his spectacles. Mutiny!

Aye, you've guessed correctly. A boat is awaitin' you. Don't miss it, or you'll be swimmin'.

And so fiction and reality joined forces and broke into Pennington-James's life. Now he had real material to write about.

They cast him ashore on a little islet strewn with boulders and rimmed with raging ocean, nothing there but low-lying scrub and gnarled, stunted trees; no fresh water, no wildlife, just sand and tea-tree amidst which Pennington-James stood forlorn in his longjohns, coughing, rubbing his toes in grey sand and feeling cold. McGann left one barrel of water and some salted pork. Pennington-James requested his logbook and quill, but was refused.

Nay, you'll be leaving no evidence of us, McGann shouted.

But just as the former captain began to scout the immediate shores of the islet, trying to remember Defoe's epic (which gave no advice of any practical nature and thus disproved the mischievous canard the author herded into the annals of real experience), there was a shout from the ship.

McGann drew himself up from the stern of the whaleboat and saw some disturbance in the water. At first he thought they were seals, but then he saw flailing, skinny arms and bobbing woolly heads swimming for shore. The captured women. The rowers needed no command. They pulled till their shoulders cracked and within a few dozen strokes were level upon the escapees. Cavalho knelt and drove a spike at the nearest and they all stopped swimming, stalled by a slight swell. McGann clouted him with the oar, knocking him over the side, but Cavalho rose and clung to the bow, blood spurting from an ear. Then the men reached over and dragged them on board, limp, exhausted. WORÉ was on her face, and when McGann turned her over he found beneath her breast a rusty stain of blood, the flapping wound turning white where the barb had entered and exited, her eyes cloudy. Waves were breaking over the bow, cold, black water frothing white, the evening murk coming upon the islands. Presently a salt mist formed and then the lashing of Bass Strait winds parted the clouds and unleashed a pale, ghostly beam of setting sun which moulded everything into a frieze of blood and boat; then into the benighted extinction of an unambiguous past.

Thus Pennington-James watched and envisaged the future. Sometimes he heard its cry, a ghostly semaphore of image and metaphor limning the sky. Sometimes an echo of a higher place, totally empty if he strove against it. But flowing, he was there and sometimes concurrently, felt the fear that he had been called. His chest pounded. A bird fluttered in his throat. His forehead ached with the effort of remaking himself. He wrung his hands together, interlaced his fingers, gesticulated at the sky. They on the ship would never see his lunging, this wrestling with invisible weights flaking with the ancient rust of indifference. There he was, cleaning and pressing, lumbering, tottering, conquering himself for the residue of individual conscience. He began rubbing two sticks together. Without pen and paper, he had a duty to survive. After the first cold tremors of the incoming night, he began to dig a hole in the scrub and laid down a glowing mat of leaves, imagining he heard above the pounding sea the snap of sail as the ship drew away forever.

In the Captain's cabin, McGann gave WORÉ a twist of valerian he kept in a small leather bag. Her spasms stopped. Then he prodded her wound with a finger dipped in whisky. She groaned, but did not cry out. It went down to the first joint of his index finger. Luckily the iron had travelled in between the ribs. No vital organs affected. He kneaded elephant-seal fat into it. The fat oozed after a while, rimmed yellow with blood and plasma. She had no fever. A sailor would be cracking a high temperature, guzzling rum, yelling with self-pity. He recognised superior health. The ship creaked and rolled. He sat through the night with her, bathing her wound, inserting a rubbery kangaroo artery as a drain, sealing and closing the wound tightly in wax. He heard the bells struck and a profound yearning came upon him. Yes, in these islands, coves, harbours, channels and inlets, he will start a tribe which will evolve in his likeness. A grand enterprise lay before him: what Napoleon had achieved through conquest, he would do by progeneration.

McGann. Paterfamilias.

Yes, he breathed into WORÉ's wounded side and mumbled words, secret, arcane and profane, sang and chanted shibboleths of long-forgotten antiphons and pronounced the hidden name upon which he would revive the glory of outcasts, strangers, the marginalia who would carry his charter into the future.

The Intercostals, he whispered, astounded by its sacramental sound.

Born with the most terrible affliction, an unrelenting sense of impending tragedy, I expected around every corner motor accidents, fatal encounters, impossible coincidences. It wasn't a fear of mortality, but of being condemned to witness it helplessly. Indeed, death would be an opportunity for relief. The day before, I pressed 200 kilograms in the Sheraton Health Club and spent the afternoon in the State Library. Dusty volumes wore me down. I choked, sneezed, sprayed like a whale. Others moved away. I read the diary of George Augustus Robinson, Administrator of the Aborigines in the 1830s. Found therein the name *McGann.* Tore out the page. So this was where Emma obtained her information.

I carried her letters in my ample pockets. Now and then, usually in the drizzle, in a moment overcome by impending tragedy, I read her garbled messages. So tenuous, these cries for help. It could all have been an elaborate joke. Indeed, just to touch her ... and then perhaps laughter would ensue between us. Merciful relief, a life of brutish heartiness. But to be challenged by silence!

Sitting on that splintered beam on the dock I had a sense of being utterly, uselessly and uncompromisingly alone. It was only a moment later that I sensed I was being watched. Behind me, in a square of water locked by a swivel bridge, jostling in the incoming tide with an assortment of crayfish boats, shrimp yawls, floating fish marts and sundry working trawlers, was an old flaking barquentine. Standing aft, leaning on the rigging, a bearded man in a peacoat and skipper's cap was regarding me closely. On the wharf, a placard advertising tours. I nodded. He spoke grudgingly, as though unused to touting for business.

We go anti-clockwise, right around.

I looked at the board. It was expensive. Do you make any stops?

Depends. For repairs.

I was intrigued. Can I come aboard?

Be my guest.

He showed me the ship. Everything was very old but extremely neat, an obsessive tidiness which went beyond that required by confined spaces. He paced the deck with deliberate and measured steps, avoiding the flat, spiral coils of rope ... Flemish Flakes, he called them ... counting out where he should stop and pointing to what would be of interest to a landsman, doing so, I thought, to gain some measure of me.

I manifested the disinterest of those to whom all was despair. Uselessness. The profound uselessness of going to sea. Only the smells fascinated me. New paint and ancient decay ... wood exuding varnish and the ceaseless effort of bodies, a wrung combination of old sweat and sapless age, of dead work and repeated renovation and of old sea-stink ... reminder of the alien element into which I felt I was already sliding.

There were three cabins, enough bed space for six to eight people, crew quarters for two, a makeshift lounge and a screwed down bar. An old diesel motor levered into a space that would have made repairs almost impossible. Sail lockers full of greasy canvas.

Down below I felt suddenly ill. Someone was trying to test the motor. KRAANG! The smell of crayfish, shell left there, on a plate. Diesel floating in off the salt ... the smell of childhood ... but no idea took hold in this loneliness of sensation. Strange how every thought goes to that, the striving for idea, in the end to make a book of life, when all the while the perfervid worm crawls slowly and ceaselessly from lithesome flesh, oozing into emptiness. I thought then of my hotel bath for some reason, the claustrophobic steaminess, no call-girl, no company to share the waters, the deliberate tortures of memory. Emma's letters. The ink running.

Once, yes, once again, in my London apartment, trying out the first of my credit ... and what better to test such an honorarium than ringing a companion, for a friend, I said, who was mute? She arrived with a card machine and I duly signed before completing the act in total silence and for the first time didn't experience the guilt of language and its betrayal. Honest sex. No images of another, except perhaps of a cancerous mole on her back, perhaps one or two twittering bats or the cry of a gull before the incoming surf. These anxieties fairly minor considering the teeming bookshelves full of them.

How old is she?

1872.

The skipper wore a black fisherman's cap, his beard silvery.

Used to do the regular run to Sydney. Built of blue gum, copper fastened, her keel stringers, waterways and strakes made in single pieces ... a superior ship, way ahead of her time ...

KRAANG!

Fuckin' be gentle with that drive shaft, will ya? Fuckin' broke one already. Fuckin' cost four hundred last time!

Turning to me, he said: Excuse me. Life on board. The colloquy of the sea. Refinement runs in the family. We've got doctors, writers, politicians. I only do this in the tourist season. Chandler. Not my name, my profession. The name's Morris.

They shook hands.

Byron.

The skipper stared at the deck.

No club foot, if you don't mind my remarking. Reminds me of my cousin. They wouldn't let him into the golf club down at Kingston. All very exclusive, you know. Then they must've felt sorry for him ... he had this disability, poor bugger ... only one arm ... and they let him join. Played immaculate golf, but once on the green kicked his ball into the hole. Used to say he had a club foot.

B.S. Johnson smiled and said: You may as well call me disabled. I worked on a trawler once and got in the way.

Yes, the sea was the last place in which he could claim any skill. It had always been the last place where others had gone before, the first to burst into that silent sea. Fouled it up for the rest. He thought Morris was pleased he wasn't one of those maritime enthusiasts for whom every clew was a matter of record.

We sail in the morning if the others turn up. You interested?

A moment of madness, secured with money, or at least ...

Byron Shelley Johnson. Mastercard.

But then the galley in which they were standing swayed. A metallic taste coated his tongue and he felt the sweating planks against his hand, the blue gum and the Huon pine and the jungle of darkness and decay and the sump of black water and bottomless gorges out of which these trunks had arisen, each from a tiny, imaginative grain. He couldn't abide it, this pinprick of light which brought coincidence close, creation and death, the crack in the wooden door in Hammersmith, the sweltering towel of childhood illness pressed against his cheek, the rancid refrain of chicken broth and the feel of his mother's cool hand; *you're not imagining it, are you, dear?* Several times he had visited that place called death by imagination, each time aboard a ship, and found a weak filament of fear through which he returned. His mother challenged him; she dared him to live and he hated it. Pale were his achievements, pallid his face, puce, the light filtering through the porthole. Evenings before departure, they used to say, made one melancholy. The waning light outlined his failures, described those hours of wrestling with God.

Morris lurched before him, coughing into the back of his hand. Told him when climbing to use two hands on the rails. One for yourself and one for the ship, he said, his right shoulder hunched, a familiar posture to those who've had tuberculosis.

It was only much later that night, when Byron Johnson found himself in a pub, his back against a weeping stone wall, that he thought about Morris's shoulder in the barque's galley, remembering again the dandruff on his peacoat, the way he coughed, the stubby fingers and the dirty notebook in which Morris McGann had pencilled in his name. That name *McGann* again.

Byron Johnson grew dizzy from drink.

Late 1820s. For over half a year they escaped detection, marauding up and down the islands of the Strait, capturing more women, killing whales, bartering sealskin. This was trade of a kind, and the British kept their eyes averted. Free enterprise, as long as it wasn't Dutch. But the *Nora* needed serious repairs and had sprung dangerous leaks.

They took the brig into the Furneaux Islands which were shrouded in mist, waves dashing against great crumbling columns of rock, erratic demons' teeth strewn half a mile out to snag those wooden butterflies of the sea. They threaded their way through channels and harbours skilfully until they found a deep-water refuge in the night, and there they drilled holes in her bottom and loaded four whaleboats with provisions and watched her go down, turning on her side and groaning like a dying whale, sending up columns of froth, soon to be nothing but swirling water and then, in the stillness, only the slow slap of oars as they made for shore.

They had cut their ties with the outside world. From now on they would speak no ship, answer no call, seek no help, raise no conventional signal.

Nights there would be fires, seen and transcribed from one island to the next, and their presence would be known, but no one would bother them (except perhaps for French explorers whom they treated with great hospitality). You see them now, hair matted, wearing kangaroo skins, sunburnt, healthy and wild-eyed, their huts in twos and threes along the coastal fringes.

Your ancestors, dear Emma. And with them, the native women, thin, lithe, food-gatherers. In the sheds, even today, they still work by oil lamps, heads in shower caps all covered in feathers, scalding, brushing and laying the muttonbirds on racks; washing, grading, sprinkling them with salt and packing them into barrels for New Zealand; pouring in brine and watching for the spud to float up when the salt was right. Maybe you'd chosen me to be the potato. Writers, I could tell you were thinking, were praters, maybe prats. But I am answering your call as a gauge of what is right.

They were left alone; silent desperados, the Intercostals, their rage directed towards their women. Yet they all survived the bleakness of the islands, not through trade but by means of their industrious concubines, who, like cobwebs placed on a wound, knitted them together. Yet they failed to have any progeny.

Once a week, as near to Sunday as he could make out for he kept no log, the bellwether of the Furneaux exhorted his tribe. Lightning rimmed the ocean. His face had thinned. The points of his broad shoulders stood out. Salt-spray formed on his brow:

> O Straitsmen, let not your isolation envelope your minds in muttonfat. Allow not listlessness to render your genitals flaccid. You have a duty towards progeny. Progeny will be the supply of labour. Progeny will be our salvation, our reward, our harvest, our rib from which we will fashion a new mankind inured to all hardship, a hybrid of the greatest intelligence, native cunning and physical strength, and through it will evolve an equal and just society. Let not this difficulty absorb you unnaturally. I suspect a trivial matter ... something we must be eating. I ... uh. We ... uh.

Spittle dribbled from McGann's chin and he lost the thread of his rhetoric, though the lightning still danced above his head and he felt a numbing absence, the loss of words when vision broke, as though the hand of God had been proffered and then withdrawn. Innovation, he had already suspected, was also dissipation. He ordered that certain vittels be eliminated from their diet and that they watch their women carefully when foraging. Half listening to him, the men turned, smirked and spat and went back to their huts to sleep.

WORÉ is still here. Three seasons older. The scar in my chest turning purple when it gets cold, standing here in the water washing myself so the seals don't smell me. WORÉ who can now speak a little in their language. She who suffers, who believes in McGann because he knows things no one else knows. He who cures illness. He who speaks at night to WORÉ the most tender of things but beats her in the morning and sometimes WORÉ approaches him out of fear as well as loyalty, wanting his praise, but out of fear and loyalty, she urinates instead.

I take the club. I walk along the edge of the water. The wind blows softly towards me. The seals snort and blow and cough. When the water is deeper, I swim quietly and reach the rocks. I climb out. Seals have poor eyesight. They scratch. I lie down on the rocks. I scratch. They sneeze. I sneeze. I let their spirit come into me. My belly is hard. I am with child. McGann can never tell. This is the third time. All he does after he squirts his seed into me is to make wax heads in my likeness. He places them all over our hut and lights the oil in them so that they glow from within. The seals beat their bellies with their flippers. I beat my belly with my fists. Hard. Harder.

There is much pain. Suddenly I jump up and hit the nearest seal with my club. It moans softly and coughs up blood. Just one blow on the snout. It dies. I take it by the flippers and drag it back to McGann, who is standing on the beach watching me. When I reach him I can see that he is in a rage.

Just one? He shouts in my ear. All that time and just one seal?

He snatches the club from my hand, jumps across the rocks holding my arm, dragging me along. I can hear my arm crack. The seals slide into the water, but for a few it is too late. McGann flails at them and in a few minutes there are five or six dying seals.

That's how you do it, he says.

But I do not understand why he wants so many to be left on the beach to stink, so the others do not return. He grabs me by the hair. Thrusts my head underwater. When I pretend I can hardly breathe, though in reality I can hold my breath for several minutes longer, he pulls me up again.

You just do it. You ask me nothing.

He holds me under again. Lifts me up.

How many pounds of seal oil can ten men produce in a single day?

Three thousand.

How long will a sixth of a pint keep a wick alight?

Twelve hours.

How do you improve the oil?

By bleeding the seal as much as possible before it dies.

Good.

He holds me under again. Another question when I rise.

What is the greatest delicacy?

The tongue.

Salted tongue! You have our tongue, WORÉ. *Then do as I say and don't play the fool. Otherwise I'll cut it out, salt it down, take it back, eat it.*

I could tell him how I killed my babies. The first one I drowned over there, by the mangrove. The second I killed by putting a firestick down its throat when it cried, in the way my people used to kill elephant seals. This one I'm killing inside me. I kill them because they will be like me. They will be women which McGann will take and thrust his seed into them. I kill them because I follow this shame which I do not yet know how to resist since I now belong nowhere. Something in me says I would prefer to die. But I am a smell on the beach, warning the others not to return. While McGann has me, there will be no more white men. The ones here grow old quickly. Then they will die too, on this white beach and one day, when there is nothing left of them, the seals will return to inhabit this place in peace.

I can see Cavalho in his hut across the bay. He's been watching all this through a spyglass which he took from a sea captain. I stick my tongue out at him and he puts down the glass and resumes what McGann calls their sexual duty. He pants and groans over my sisters. When he is spent and asleep, they will mix into his stew the seal liver they have been extracting and they will mince the pulp of grass trees into his tea and day by day he will grow more stupid and he will vomit and shit continuously. Too busy watching McGann trying to drown me, he hasn't seen the ship on the horizon coming towards us.

Time shrouds everything; pares down speech; makes life black or white.

Must've been that seeping pub wall. Moisture down the vertebrae causing unwanted connections. Some sort of short-circuit in the brain. They told me I was flailing about at the bar; no mere drunkard, not the DT's either, someone had experience of that. An ex-rugbyman from the St John's Ambulance, a Knight-Hotelier, thrust a blackjack into my mouth to prevent lockjaw after hitting me about the head first a few times to elicit ingenuousness.

The next morning I had mostly recovered.

Apparently I'd slept out, on the lawn beside the CSIRO building in Hobart. I can remember periods of consciousness, watching the fishing fleet go out at two in the morning, lights flickering, the bottle of Guinness in my left pocket, the fuzzy grass, smell of the world spinning beneath.

For over a year, Byron Johnson suffered from not being himself. That was the trouble. He thought he was going mad, but other people assured him he was simply drifting a little. Which was far from the truth. This was a huge worry. He thought he had a grip on it and then it slipped like a fish from the hand. Still, a pleasure that another self had regained life. That he worried the truth was escaping him meant he wasn't mad. Yet. And so he had discovered a solution of sorts. He clung to the belief that metaphysics meant you weren't mad. Transcendentalism was sanity in a sordid, disappointingly real world. Then he discovered silence. But the trouble with that was when he did speak, something gushed involuntarily with excess.

For a while, at parties, he nodded wisely, he nodded foolishly. He didn't think it really mattered, until the night the celebrated publisher Elaine Friedman launched her first novel. She flushed him out. You think my novel's shit, don't you? she asked. He nodded. It wouldn't have mattered had she not broken her wineglass over his head and made the morning papers. He knew they had already surpassed him, these first-timers. They were in tune with issues. They moved on ... and trampled over him. Oh, yes, Byron S. Johnson, once a legatee of Beckett and Joyce. Now maybe a character in one of their books. Silence meant he had nothing to say; yesterday's man again. Yet when the Other Self performed, what a toll it took! Each exaggeration a painful tattoo on his back he was condemned to wear forever. Word for word and word by word the public mocked him.

And of course he fell in love with Elaine Friedman and had to more than once accommodate her husband, the cantankerous New York publisher D.V. Ravisingh, who really did turn things in his favour. He was back in circulation briefly. He made fruitful collaborations, but his real work suffered. The building of integrity had to do with reserve, retrieval and balance. That was before he married Ainslie Cracklewood. She set him on the path of no return. Moved him into an apartment of his own and, like George Sand, shielded and prodded him by turn and forced him to get on with it. Then to add the tragedy he had always needed, left him.

I smelled the grass and dreamt how once, near here, they brought convicts to be hung, and here once they set out on an expedition, a thin black line of death to kill every native they could find; here a place of fish and blood, and here too, the beginning of great adventures: Mawson leaving from yonder Queen's Pier, to dare the hummocks and treacherous floes; here whalers set sail and spent winters locked in ice long before maps were made, maps in which sometimes a gaping hole appeared. That's when they needed a third eye to stare down fear ... the moment when they stepped outside their own creation.

It had always been harder for introverts to stare down fear. We had an upstart teacher who was reading Freud. He tried to teach us the terms. In Hammersmith, in primary school, we ran naked on sports days by the Thames, escaping Tunnel Ball and dragging dead cats from the sludge, sluicing flotsam in search of buried hulks or lost watches, and sticking our fingers into one another's navels, shouting innies or outies? Pressing hard until a nervous reflex of pain made the victim squirm. Innies were introverts. They felt pain. They had this hole in the centre of themselves, no evidence of a true parting from their mothers. But they were more than the merely human.

Even before the womb, a desire for inanimateness.

But the third eye of the introverts saw victory beyond death. Those who possessed it fell, always a sacrifice so others would be saved. In every age they go forth, sensitivities bared, the burghers of history ... mad, masochistic, dangerously extreme. Our Freudian teacher was dangerously extreme. He massaged the backs of our necks as he walked up and down the aisle of the bus, consumed by Freud. My mother said he could get dismissed for that kind of thing.

Well, down to the sea in ships. The barque *Nora* looked good in the sunlight and Morris was there, scampering among the rigging with simian arms. A gymnast once, perhaps. He was waving. Damn. Will have to wave back. Didn't think old salts did that kind of thing. Finally glad he didn't wave back. Morris was winching something up. Didn't see the rope. The fitted out boat looked too complicated. Two other men appeared and disappeared. Surly types, cigarettes in mouth, beanies on their heads. Nobody spoke. This was good.

He went down to his cabin hoping to meet the other passengers but none had arrived. Chose the upper bunk, pulled back the sheets just in case. Old school habit. Prison the same. You survived the snoring on top, but not the insomniacs. Insomniacs smoked. He went on deck and observed some of the action. Took a few mental notes of how they prepared the sails. Didn't have to be an expert to see things that began to ring alarm bells, for they were either taking short cuts or counting on the weather to be fine throughout, which was highly unlikely. They made do with one squaresail yard crossed on the fore and a small aft rig and he wasn't feeling any better when he saw the drums of diesel the two deckhands were hauling aboard. It wasn't going to be plain sailing, but a kind of motorised subsidy. The *Nora* must have been inefficient to windward, so he was glad he didn't choose the cabin over the steerage.

He went back down, spread some of his things over the lower bunk and made his way to the engine housing. Motor installed in 1950, the plate once riveted to the side hanging loose. He found a bottle of beer on the shelf, pried it open, sat down near the shaft and studied the starter motor. The hydraulic accumulator charged by a belt-driven pump. No hand lever in case the pressure dropped. Judging by the water in the bilge, there was a fair amount of leakage from the shaft housing. The beer smelled like old socks and tasted warm, so he left most of it, then thought he'd better get rid of it and poured it down an empty oil drum, which, come to think of it, looked like a fuel tank. Nothing seemed quite as shipshape as before. He looked under the cowling. Found a metal box. Took something from it and put it into the pocket of his jacket. He went up on deck and climbed down onto the dock.

Felt better when a luxury limousine pulled up and a couple got out and walked towards the *Nora*. The man was stocky, wearing sunglasses and a leather jacket. He had long greasy hair, an earring in his left earlobe. Possibly a rock musician. They kept some distance between them. She had upper class written all over her; conservative but expensive dress, supercilious expression, blow-job mouth, tanned and well-shaped legs you wouldn't often see out of jodhpurs. He'd learned the smell from Ainslie. It took one look at them to tell him the gigolo married her for property. The fellow made his fingers into a pistol.

Hi. You crew or passenger?

He didn't like the familiarity, so he pointed back in like manner, a Mexican stand-off perhaps, indicating they were all in the same boat, *compadre*. He nodded. Looked at the wife.

Gotcha, the husband said.

She had just a whisper of contempt on her face. Enough to say: Kiss my arse, buster.

Gladly, but not yet.

It took a little time to realise the disdain was reserved for her husband. Then when she stepped over the threshold into her above-deck cabin, she glanced very quickly around. His heart pumped. A long time. It had been a long time. He feared the old flaws.

Next couple arrived. Mr and Mrs Average. Made him feel at home. He in checked flannel shirt and lumberjacket, she in trackpants and parka. They had won well at the casino. Raked in at the tables and the cruise was part of the deal — getting off at Launceston for another fling. He could imagine them standing all day at the roulette table in their sandals, faces so innocent no one could tell they'd been winning for three days and when they settle up she could hardly lug the chips out of her bag. They should have gone back to Queensland, set up a gas-grog-and-go store on the corner of some dusty highway, but they always wanted more and pretty soon they would slide down the other side when the luck ran out. And it always did. He'd seen his father do that; the Johnsons had never known what to do with an oil spout in their own backyard. Moving house was the traditional response. Here they were in another guise. Mr and Mrs Mitchell-Smith. The hyphen came with the luck.

The *Nora* got under weigh at noon, making for Port Arthur. They would all spend the night at the penal settlement in a motel a manacle's throw from some of the bleakest dormitories in the Antipodes.

It is, as usual, WORÉ who first sees the barque and the Union Jack she had been taught to fear. The ship is coming in fast, close-hauled, and she can see a man on the bowsprit taking fathoms.

Three ... two and a half.

McGann, who is chasing her, walloping her with an open hand, stops when she suddenly stops shrieking.

Sperm! Ship!

Two ... two.

Silence comes over the whole of the island. The plovers and the redbills and the muttonbirds all go to ground. Seals slip slowly into the water eyes rolled back in fear. McGann passes a hand over his brow, sees that there is no time, remains rooted to the sand.

One and a half.

Suddenly ...

Shit!

He hears the cry first, then sees that the man on the bowsprit has fallen into the water. They've hit a sandbank. The sails luff, but they manage to come about. Now they will have to drop a longboat for him.

McGann seizes the moment, moves quickly and invisibly along the rocks, blows a blast through his cupped palms and almost immediately men are herding their women through the scrub, hiding them in grass, burying them in sand, reminding them that if they show, the British will have them do needlework and read the bible and cage them up for these activities, spikes around their necks. This message entrenched with occasional beatings and slavish incantations ... Oh, ye children of disaffiliation, McGann would croon, repeat after me ...

They were well rehearsed. One or two ran vines into their hair and popped up camouflaged in the distance, invisible even to the cheeky seabirds wheeling and nagging over the bluff to examine the ship for offal.

They had, by now, picked up the fathomer, rope still wrapped around his wrist.

Half! I said half! he spluttered.

The ship had dropped anchor, chain running echoes along the cliff-face. Shouts. More longboats swinging beneath the davits. Sounds not heard in years. Cavalho loaded the muskets. Through his spyglass he could see McGann lighting a dozen wax-heads fixed on stakes in inlets and hidden coves, a kind of pagan ritual at first glance, but he knew the wax melted in time to light the gunpowder compacted in the shafts, soon to give the impression of a hundred guns. Foolishness, to be sure, against cannon the barque was undoubtedly carrying, but these would be precious minutes of chaos to mask their escape in whaleboats which would thread through shallows to another isle.

The longboat grounded. Two marines are thrown forward, looking sheepish, stumbling ahead of the incoming surf. Waxheads glimmering in the mist.

Don't look good, Sir. Them taboos terrifyin' me.
Fear not, son. Them is white man's devilry.

Southern swells waking from the ocean bed. One who looked like their leader steps off the bow and sinks his leather shoe into the grey sand. The sand is soft. He sinks up to his calves. Water seeps into his silk stockings, up his satin breeches, splashes his red coat, sash and various decorations. He has on an enormous penis gourd, the tip of which is held up with string fastened around his neck. For over four years he has lived amongst the natives, travelled up and down and through their lands, slept with their women, scratched himself raw on freezing nights wrapped in wallaby skin and layers of fat and lice. He knew the penis gourd impressed them. The Great White Father. He adjusts himself; winces at the gonorrhoeal itch-and-sting in his groin. Sniffs the air and says: Bastards!

We were milling around the small bar housed in the main cabin mid-way along the deck, getting to know each other under the generous influence of alcohol, when the toffee-nose, Julia her name was, let fly with a few historical banalities. She reminded me of an actress, I don't know why, perhaps there was a very slight resemblance to Ainslie, whose curls gave her a child's aura when she spoke her lines and made every critic feel like a paedophile. But Julia was much more professional. She had a hard edge to her voice. Perhaps aspirants had to try harder. I thought about actresses. Thought about movies. Maybe Julia was in movies. I gathered she lived on a big property in the north-west. I wanted to talk about movie stars; how they coped with nude love scenes. They never mention it, even in avenging memoirs, how they managed the foreplay and the simulated sex and then picked up their dough and said goodbye till the next film. Did they work off before the shoot, take valium? Go with the flow? Shower with ice cubes?

George Augustus Robinson, Julia said, sailed these waters gathering up indigenous people planning to house them on the Tasman peninsula. (Here she crooked a finger at the cliffs off the port bow. She sounded like a tour guide.) He sailed up to the Furneaux trying to rescue the women from the sealers in order to settle them on Flinders Island.

The Mitchell-Smiths went, Hmmmm. Interesting.

Bravo, I said. But George Robinson was really an upstart bricklayer.

She looked across at me.

What he did was as bad as killing them off. He institutionalised them to death. In fact ...

She was blushing, drinking her vermouth in one long swallow.

He was a whitewash. He existed to temper everyone's guilt.

Julia pinched a strand of hair from her mouth. I had touched a sore point, hypocrite that I was, who, devoted to sense, was nevertheless blowing smoke. I revelled in the gaps between historical furores. Once at a literary festival I was asked about my devotion to truth ... whether I went with narrative history or temporality or the genealogical tradition. All three, I replied, but only if you lived it yourself. I was generous, even affluent then. I could afford a joke at my own expense. In humanities departments this became no laughing matter. Professors soon wrote me off as a joke. I was no longer a serious novelist. That too, is a way of coming to the truth, to life, to what is necessary, without artifice.

Julia's husband/lover/gigolo rubbed his earring. Morris was having a great time, looking from one face to another.

Well, I was getting to that, Julia said primly. Whatever the case, Robinson had good intentions.

I let that pass to oil the waters. Morris looked disappointed. I asked Julia where she lived. She sensed a trap, but answered gamely.

Northmere.

I saw Morris frown. He knew what that name meant: the huge pastoral leases of the Van Diemen's Land Company. The north-west corner of this foreign field where Aborigines mysteriously disappeared. The clean air monitoring station. Cape Grim.

By the way, Julia said, thinking she was holding a trump card, I'm a descendant of Robinson's.

Everybody held their breath. I wasn't shocked. All I thought of was Robinson's diary:

> *Wybalenna Aboriginal Settlement*
> *Flinders Island*
> *Monday, 23rd November 1835.*

Robinson is out walking with Mrs Dickenson, the storekeeper's wife. That evening he writes:

> *Mrs D. REE. DEVERY my.*

He likes ciphers. Studied signals and codes once. Not so difficult really, if you knew the Aboriginal words as he did. Wrote it in upper case. *VULVA!* Erupting like a volcano from its coded compactness. And later:

> *Mrs D. in the evening my PAGENNA.*

KISS! came the confession of foreplay as an afterthought, Robinson of the cunningly retrogressive pen, as if thought precluded action. Robinson of the good intentions.

But let's burn some bird fat and barilla and wash out our mouths. Robbo was a writer.

I didn't trump Julia. I let her smile linger. She denied me in a kind of reversal of what I knew. She denied me the truth. At one stage ... I cannot remember now when it occurred ... perhaps after the burning whisky had loosened my face, collapsed the rictus of marmoreal cynicism ... she asked me how old I was.

Too old, I had answered, but not old enough for suicide. (Yes, self-preservation had a distinctly erotic nature.) Yet hers was a strange question. I fleetingly imagined how it would feel to be loved by her, but my weakness for the death-wish manifested itself. I expected her to say something further, for she seemed to enjoy my prognosis a great deal.

So with the sea, with adventure, the intangibles became clear. I believe she could have saved me. I could smell excitement, a dimension of life I thought had passed forever. A dark shape slid beneath the ship.

We sailed close to the imposing cliffs, pipes and flutes like a grand organ, erosion working stone into frightening pinnacles topped with bird lime, and rode the light swell into Port Arthur. It was very calm in there, the water dark and the ruins of the penitentiary glowing pink like a burning mansion, a crumbling, porous cake of wormy expectation. Dusk must have woven something magical. I expected Julia to make another sign ... some courtly concern for passion. I kept staring at her and became trapped. I think she was frightened. The light fell in different layers on her and there was this kaleidoscope of colours working on her face as she turned, the moving landscape behind veiled in shades, and she became an imposing Madonna carried on the backs of swaying priests. Things began to whirl inside my head and I withdrew and Julia carried the evening, won everybody. As for me, I had escaped just in time. The Other was capable of so much sound and fury.

I think I could have lived off scandal for years if I had kept up with the Julias and Ainslies of this world ... made public banal love stories about broken hearts, desperation wrung from a glance, the touch of fingers in the afternoon light. But the clothes soon drop and in brazen nudity the Other and I would have lectured the world long after it had stopped listening. Better the false step now ... the indiscretion, the violation. Between that and the veil, practical philistinism. A lobotomy of sorts.

Her husband found Morris in the engine room. He knew something about diesel motors. That was all I needed to free myself to think of Julia all night, to have her while Morris and her husband repaired the engine I had unwittingly sabotaged earlier that morning. I waited at the stern for the painter. Unfurled a torn page of Robinson's diary to pass the time. The year was 1830.

Robinson walked up and down the gravelly beach on the first of these islands to be liberated, Union Jack held aloft behind him, a lieutenant following with a basket of food. He stopped periodically, placed a hand on the shoulder of a valet, removed his shoe and shook out the sludge.

Hello! Anybody about?

There was nothing.

He walked on, irritated, snatching up the smouldering wax heads and dousing them in the water.

Perfidy! he shouted.

They reached the huts. Robinson entered one; came out scratching.

Fleas, he said.

Sandfleas covered his legs. He bent to slap at his calves and the tip of the gourd poked him in the eye.

Shit!

There was an irrational moment when he wanted to torch the huts. His men seemed to sense this and came forward with firebrands. Robinson waved them away. Better to threaten than to antagonise. He picked up a smooth rock he found in the fireplace and tacked a notice on the centrepost of the largest hut: *All Native Women to be returned to the Authorities at earliest convenience.* He spun around on his heel, strode back to the longboat.

Wha' 'bout the hamper, Sir? asked the lieutenant.

Poison it. Goddamn, man, this is no picnic.

Within an hour they had rowed back to the cutter. When the ship disappeared on the outgoing tide, Cavalho whistled up the women. They tested the roast chicken in the basket on a cat. Within minutes it lay writhing, convulsing, its eyes red and bursting from its head. Cavalho snatched off the decree. None of them could read save McGann, who had already sailed west in a four-ton whaleboat. Cavalho tore up the parchment and, crazed with hunger for chicken, chewed on the fragments.

Byron Johnson had the common but unfortunate affliction of seeing himself speak and therefore experiencing the excitement of the object of love slipping away in the balloon of dialogue. It would have resembled Montgolfier's craft. Lifting off on hot air. But how sweet the pain! How defiant of gravity! Whenever he felt love, even in the emptiness of letters (whose distance *made* it love, yes, love was absence, always a *wanting* ... to express and to die), he sought out another as surrogate, with whom he would make metaphors instead of love. Uncomprehending strangers became his obscure object of desire; they unwittingly protected him from the pain of the original slippage. But of course, there was a penance for this ... parody; sometimes revenge; even love itself.

Except for the ruins of the penitentiary, Port Arthur presented nothing extraordinary to him. Tasmania, heralding itself as the Holiday Isle made much of this volcanic peninsula joined naturally by the narrowest neck of land. It made much of history. It even afforded the same tutored views of England ... headlands and sea, trees and rocky coastlines which, viewed from one lookout to the next, brought upon him a mild exhaustion, for he had been told time and again what Countryside and Beauty and Wilderness were. He'd seen them on cans of air-freshener. Forever sentenced to a displaced Nature, standing on the edge of a lookout like a hanging verb, the English mind, with its hatred of cities, brought a clumsy intimacy to a horrifying aesthetic. The beauty of transportation was that isolation purified the soul. Men were reformed to innocence.

So the penal settlement, the institutionalised viciousness of the past, remained the one true repository of anticipation for present-day tourists, its gloom powdered with English lawns, mouldering stones and melancholic trees, its savagery residing only in popular mythology and imaginings ... if not for the human toil which produced all of it, rubbed everything with elbow grease and brow sweat and bloodied back, polished every block and beam, all the iron accoutrements, every leathern boot and wooden stock and soaked every cap and whip in blood in the service of the motherland. So eager were the condemned in the end to find the promised nirvana of animals, they gave up even momentary life for sweet, sweet death by going down to the sea or into the forest.

In the painter, which could only ferry three people at a time, Ms Julia Dickenson was heard to say to Mrs Mitchell-Smith that she fancied a ghost-tour, for that was the speciality of the evening. The Commandant's residence came into view as the dusk submerged into night. For Byron Johnson, there was always a moment at that critical juncture when light met darkness, when the heart crossed from melancholy to illicit arousal. A little flutter, irregularly on the cardiograph. But at that very moment a crow glided across the velveteen lawns and nagged its way across a line of trees, landing with heavy, slow beatings of its wings. For Byron Johnson, a presentiment. Ah, scavenging heart ... he said, poring over the rubble of a ruthless time, the dead watching the winter coming on with admirable disinterest ... I'm outside of it all again. But no one was there to listen. Just as well, for a strange laughter erupted across the harbour and foam curled on the crests of waves and there was the beginning of a gentle fit.

A creamy cottage, its warm light astride the lawn, welcomed the ladies. Lamps lit the path. Across Eaglehawk Neck they saw bonfires and heard the baying of hounds. Up at the church, carriages disgorged huddles of people which soon disbanded and disappeared. Coaches rounded the drives and there were little shouts of Get up! and Whoa! and the scrunching of hooves over gravel. Pines swooned menacingly in the strengthening wind.

Morris returned, casting his oars expertly between waves. The gentlemen came next.

I think, Mrs Mitchell-Smith said, adjusting her bonnet, that we should need a stout arm on this tour. I'm often subject to frights and faintings.

Oh, but there'll be plenty of *them,* Julia Dickenson said.

The latter was far more experienced in these matters and was already looking for the unwelcome presence, which came in the form of Alf Mitchell-Smith and that detestable Byron Johnson, who was chewing on a bit of paper. Julia's husband and the Captain had decided to stay on board.

They all walked up the path, the ladies ahead, to the Commandant's cottage. Two sisters had turned it into a guesthouse, and there they were, Adèle and Aimée, one grave, one acute, fluttering like ageing moths in new light, ordering servants and porters about, instructing the cook and turning down featherbeds. They were twins, one in red and one in blue, long dresses brushing over gravel, stepping sideways through doors, whalebone swimming beneath velvet.

Ahoy! they sang in unison. What ho, agreeable visitors?

There were twin murals on either side of the portico, some Grecian or Egyptian fancy which fired the romantic past despite their last lover abandoning them, yes, after a lucid explanation that he could only satisfy one at a time and like Solomon, drew a sword to his manly parts, hoping to have love declared by one or the other, but both twins urged him on, impressed. Never mind that it had been so long ago that the murals were flaky from sea salt and were melting into ancient absences. Never mind that the story, so oft repeated at dinners with the utmost propriety, yet with a hint, just the slightest, of prurience, the story of their god-like lover, may have been interwoven with Homer's. For his name was Paris. No, it may have happened in Paris. What? Oh, Aimée, such audacity! Our guests, remember?

By then a cloth had quickly been laid and there was hot soup and a roast and wine, then coffee with the most exquisite cream and a fire crackling in the hearth as the evening grew cool and the guests chattered on, Adèle and Aimée providing the stories through the spell of their voices, the quaint pronunciation, the rustling sibilants and lilting vowels inducing a coma. They told of the Commandant's wife, of how her ghost had recently reappeared in the rocking chair in the back room, by the fire. But they did not know why she had returned to haunt the house, nor whether she was an evil woman, nor whether some sadness lay unresolved.

All ghosts are lonely. And banal, and secretive. A reflection of our scourge when we are not at one with ourselves, Byron Johnson interrupted.

The others frowned. A terrible man, this Johnson. Intruded all the time. Claimed to be a writer, but none had heard of him. That's the trouble with such aspiration ... nothing but constant chafing.

But there were other ghosts, other stories of runaway convicts ... of Pearce, whose name was on everybody's lips ... Pearce, who escaped from Sarah Island in Macquarie Harbour, who made it through the wilderness, the rainforests, the impregnable walls thick with tanglefoot and mined with ravines, made it through gorges and the jungle of Huon pine, myrtle and celery-top, swinging on vines across hanging swamps and strangulated sassafras, walking for a mile without setting foot on the ground over fallen swamp gum and giant moss-bound roots and gangrenating undergrowth; Pearce, who made it by eating his fellow escapees; Pearce, who was caught and escaped again, running naked on a beach near Hell's Gates, posing and proposing lyrically to his mate that grace was dying for another ... real passion; indolently whispering in his ear; seen running again, alone this time, hailing a passing whaleboat.

Pierre-s, Adèle said.

Pierre-s, Aimée echoed. A terrible man.

But it was different here.

Yes, here it was more civilised.

They were mentally trained, not often physically punished.

Yes, they were isolated.

According to Bentham's theory.

Every prisoner watched.

Without him seeing that he was so.

Silence was the golden rod.

Silence and observation.

Observation and silence.

A modern concept.

Conceived in darkness.

Executed in light.

Each cell dank, with thick walls.

For self-examination.

So others could not hear, save the gaoler of the self.

Creative solutions to stifle creativity.

Training the mind to ritual.

To dissymmetry.

I and my fellow man.

All unequal depending on one's time.

Wooden boxes like coffins in chapel.

Chapel boxes so they can't see each other.

Just man and God.

The scourge of solidarity.

The eye of Humanism.

In the eye of the Law, just parts.
Balanced shares.
Shared balance.
Punishment without pain.
Contrition within time.
Supervision.
Codes.
A refuge from disorder.
One man took off his hand.
Perhaps it was gangrenous.
And said: Put that in yer stew.
We are our own worst enemy.
Janus-faced.
Good and evil.
Evil and good.
You can hear them stirring now.
Turning about, to and fro, muttering.
Isolated, internalised.
Trying to find remorse.
In the end, just ghosts.
Just voices.
Justice.

Which suddenly reminded the twins of the purpose of all this. They leapt up, looking at the clock. The ghost tour!

I will be a guide, said Adèle.

And I too, said Aimée. Therefore we shall split into two parties. But you will see the same things. Mrs D., I can see by the way you stand that you are anxious. Real ghosts are not malicious.

Julia Dickenson and Byron Johnson. They were picked in the same group, much to the consternation of

Mrs Mitchell-Smith who thought it unfair. Julia chewed on a corner of her handkerchief.

Boom! Something knocked against the hull of the ship and echoed across the water. A presentiment, Byron Johnson said. Her anxiety a denial. Boom! Her seriousness a refutation. He wanted to kill the child in him, that provocation to diversion. Boom! The twin guides separated the dark with their lanterns, poled along forked paths at a similar pace beneath ancient trees contorted by wind. Boom again. From the ruins a groaning, a low murmur. A few drops of salted rain. Pitch black now, as Julia Dickenson and Byron Johnson lingered behind while one twin talked, another reminisced, made incantations to an unknown soldier in a forgotten war, answered herself, then they answered each other beyond the hedge with words preserved like ginger or ashes in a jar stowed in memory bright as day; otherwise the grey truth in the loquacious presence of madness.

Julia held her silence. He smelt her perfume, the fragrance of what could have been; a smile, flashing eyes, subtlety, the intermarrying of minds. Boom! Already the gossip spread by Adèle and Aimée of Julia entering the guard tower, having been detached from the rest of the party which came together below it, escaping that detestable Johnson. How she was wandering in the dark when something struck her face ... a bat? How she fled but couldn't find the others, scurrying up and down slopes and paths and stone steps, hearing her voice echoing and then nothing but a terrifying moan from somewhere deep in the isolation cells, convicts whispering:

Arrrgh! Let's play Chinese Whispers.

What's that?

Don't you know? Didn't you play it as a child?

I had no childhood.

That's what they all say.

All right. Stop arguing. I'll spread a rumour. You pass it on to the next. Let it do the rounds and then back to me and I'll report it to all of you.

What's the point?

To see the difference. To tell the truth about lies. To see that justice is never done. To illustrate the jury system.

Ah! a good game.

'Tisn't a game.

You are what they say you are.

Chinee whispers, Chinee whispers.

You! Cell number ten! Why aren't you playing?

Go fuck yourself.

Oh! Julia blushed, holding in her hand a tourist brochure, a magazine, a map, a bookmark printed with the times and meeting-places of tour parties. But it was too dark to read the:

Notes on contributors:

Cell no.1 :	
John Thomas :	25 years for self-abuse.
Cell no. 2:	
Ernest Pleasure:	2 years for homicidal rape.
Cell no. 3:	
Marcus Green:	20 years for hawking with intent to expectorate on the King. Author of *The*

	Everyman's Guide to Port Arthur's Panopticon.
Cell no. 4:	
Sam 'Boon' Halliday:	25 years for recidivism. Original crime unknown. His study of the Huon Pine was funded by the Van Diemen's Volk Group.
Cell no. 5:	
Chris Femfresh:	5 years for impersonation. Is working on a book on gender and confusion and was most recently awarded the Commandant's Prize for good behaviour.
Cell no. 6:	
Joseph Nill:	Published work includes a collection of short stories and the novels *Absence* and *Nothing*. He is a reconstructed escapist.
Cell no. 7:	
Rodney Pearce:	Brother of the famous cannibal from Sarah Island. On bread and water diet.
Cell no. 8:	
Simon Solomon:	20 years for forgery. Has worked as a journalist and arts editor of the *V.D. Times*. His publications

	include *Oh, Plagiarism!* and *Why Are We In Port Arthur?* He is currently working on an experimental novel without punctuation, entitled *Will The Sentence Ever End?*
Cell no. 9:	
Charlie Challenger:	50 years to life for being black. A member of the Ben Lomond tribe, Charlie published a pamphlet on English immigration which was deemed to be inflammatory. It was pulped in 1848.
Cell no. 10:	
Wilson Ho:	A Chinese-born writer stranded in Port Arthur.

Oh! Boom! Julia flees. She runs from the cells and steps out into the rain, into the arms of Byron Johnson, who, taking advantage of the dark, kisses her firmly on her half-open lips.

Oh, Ms D. REE. DEVERY, my, oh my! he exclaims.

What? Asks a startled voice from cell number 9.

I must have been quite drunk that night, eating alone in the motel dining-room ... three empty bottles stood on the table, toppling over when I managed to get up. Thought they would have taken them away to alleviate the embarrassment at least. I was full of spleen, though they say you can do without it. Suddenly hated myself, the suddenness of it getting to me, not the familiarity of its occurrence. The long, empty sentences of the night; the blowing in bottles; shuffling swill of sea at my feet; my life made fit for other people's words. I was sick of it. I wanted Emma to hold in my arms, not feel her pages rustling beneath me. I groped along the wall to my room; didn't see Julia D. at all, but passing, heard groans from intermittently occupied rooms, long, unstaunched suffering so often confused with practised ecstasy. Take no pride in solitude. To love, you must have fact! Another. But through savagery or treaty, the worm of solitude is already in the heart at birth ... though mighty deeds have sprung from the microfilaria of loneliness. In passing. That deadly move in chess which picks off the isolated with indifference. I looked for a gymnasium. There was none. I tried her door.

Morning. Raining lightly outside. Port Arthur veiled in glassy mists sweeping sideways in fierce wind gusting from the sea. Cold rain. Puff. Puffing. Penance for taking everything too lightly. I set off on a slow jog, not knowing where I was going, puff, preparing, though prisons have circular exercise yards, surprised at the iciness of this rain, puff, the cold slick of the road, long and black, so lonely and deep, the colour. I'm prepared to run forever, puff, the arduous dips and crests hardly noticeable at first, but each breath registering some degree of death, the pain so subtle, maybe round the corner the swaying caravan of some crazed camper will flatten me like a possum, puff, steep now, almost sheer, turn right onto a dirt road climbing into fog, ascending Calvary, the cross of this weighty body, puff, trees black, sky black, too Olympian, this pace, still refusing respite, the beat of blood drives a numbed mind past some cleared land and a farmhouse, bark of a startled terrier, thinking of you then, Emma, perhaps indecently, the sway of your walk, the way you fold your thin arms beneath the sweater draped over your shoulders, just like Julia ... the sadness of your eyes, perhaps the sweetness of your breasts, of which I can only guess, no, puff, the bleak score of heath between heavy and scanty vegetation in these climes, puff, member shrunken to a champignon with this Herculean effort, near the top now, each step the loosening of gravel, feet sodden by runnels, the tide of arterial blood in my ear, I've gone to water, puff, will not give in, can hear the brief thunder of startled kine, the summit: die, die.

Ho! What blows? A meadow soft with the fuzz of rain-smeared flowers. Out there, look, the harbour. Neap tide. Point Puer. Pronounced 'pure', though Latinists (but not dyslectics) would disagree. The suspicion of pederasty, but much worse, the stink of hypocrisy. Boys. They transported boys here, placed them on an outcrop and watched them wither and die while making shoes and boats, in cretinous mimicry of God the Economist, of labour and debt, of Service to the King, in one of the most severe climes in the world ... watched them shiver ... here, a telescope ... twenty cents for half a minute of horror. How many dashed themselves from the cliffs? Sheer, no shortfall if a few dozen slipped quietly down, heads split on submerged rock and then the slow diffusion of a tide incarnadine. Breathe in. The smell of coffinwood and weed, pungent with age and dankness, whips across the bay. A wormy attitude in the best views. All those attitudes wrought of soured breaths in all those small-minded ways of proud ancestry whispered to us in the night. Yet in childhood, having been told of glorious deeds, we were locked in rooms for essaying them, refused the air-raid shelter and dared to wet the bed in excitement. We told the time by bending the hands of the clock, watching the days by the movement of the sun across the walls, suffer-ing enuresis in the soft flare of bombs at night and dwelt in recurrent dreams, so as not to miss any part of the show. Hearing the sirens of frightened men, Father with a newspaper and matches in his warden's helmet, torched our sheets, the soft 'phutt' of saturated linen refusing to burn our sins away when during his rage, murderous rage, he hoped we would all perish in the chaos.

Here, let me discard these trappings of the past. Here, strip naked; football jumper, shorts, socks. Standing on this rock and holding my arms outstretched, I gesture to She who makes all things possible. Oh, Magna Mater, deliver me from Elohistic mysteries, call me by my own name. Let me live simply, without meaning.

I'm cold. I try to run down a little. Catch my foot in a hole. Stumble.

On an isolated, tiny island two years after the brig *Nora* disappeared, George Robinson, self-appointed Aboriginal agent and master of the Wyballenna settlement, sighted a naked white man running along the beach waving a smoking branch. He sent a boat to pick up the castaway. The man stank. He was unable to speak. They put him in quarantine. He coughed up blood and looked to be dying. He indicated he wanted pen and paper and began to scribble illegibly with a shaking hand.

> My name is Orville Pennington-James, erstwhile master of the brig '*Nora*' which was taken from me by a mutinous crew. I was cast on that island and left to die. I didn't, as you can see. Some native women paddled across in a bark canoe every week with stolen provisions, filched, I guessed, from white men. Well, I've learned a feckin' thing or two about native women. My father always said that I would ...

At this point his hand fell and ink spilled across his chest. Blood bubbled from a corner of his mouth. Writing had been such an immense effort that he suddenly lost all desire for it and began wrestling with a knot deep in his chest, dreaming of a dark woman who suckled him.

WORÉ has a knot in her chest. Right here. All night she coughs inside her bark shelter. All night the terrible sound she has never heard before: a high-pitched whine, phlegm erupting at the end of it, a string of tiny explosions like bursting sutures. That's what she has seen McGann do ... sew up the wounds in the bodies of men he'd killed, the bodies expanding and stinking, bloated by sunlight and then ... the sound of bursting sutures. He studied them, measured their chests, placed wax over their faces; sealed their mouths. He would take a sharp needle, the kind for making sails. Go down to the third or fourth space between the ribs. Pierce the flesh. Insert a larger needle in the weal. All the way in. Watch as the cloudy fluid seeped out. A hiss of gas.

If he were here he would have studied this cough, listened with his ear to her chest. But now he has gone to fetch more women. Perhaps he will not be back. WORÉ has a child in her belly ... but something tells her it cannot be ... like a wallaby with two heads, it just cannot be.

She goes down by the water, immerses herself. The pain returns. She has a fit of coughing, her heart moving in her chest, beating in her throat at times and below that an emptiness, a falling. This, her mother had told her, was an experience of death. After that there is no more fear. She coughs, lips smeared in blood. She wades out into deeper water. It is cold. The pain comes like the waves. Slowly, then terribly when it hits and then mercifully recedes and returns more rapidly than before. WORÉ stays in the water. She floats, she pushes, squeezes. She is filled with a murderous joy. There are spasms. A trembling. Then quite easily, something comes. She can see it through the water, white and trailing blood and umbilical and bits of her insides and she grows dizzy and makes one last effort, suddenly grabbing it like a fish and holding it under with great love and gentleness and keeping it there for all eternity.

Cavalho sees her, rushes down to the water and understands what she is doing. He takes her by the hair and drags her out of the sea and sees that she is choking on blood. He pitches her onto the sand, the dead baby with her. He is too late. WORÉ's eyes are glassy, her legs awash with dark blood which pumps out, deep red, purple. Cavalho sits down and howls. Doesn't know why he is doing it, but hears a wondrous sound emerge from his throat. Feels all alone.

Something else floats in the amniotic sea. Cavalho wipes away his tears, rushes back into the water, raises it up. A twin! She had delivered twins and had missed one, which he hurriedly transports to one of his concubines, to Worrete-Moete, who had milk. Cavalho disappears for a while, then returns; toys with a little package, a ball of wax.

A week later, assured that the baby would survive, Cavalho and his men fire the grasses. They burn down the huts, destroy what they cannot carry and sail off, the whole island alight, singed muttonbirds caught in their burrows darting into the sea, others, aflame, exploding in mid-air, spiralling on short wings like fizzing cannonballs.

An exemplary life is one that prepares for the perfection of its own death.

That was the last thing Byron Johnson ever wrote. He was in his cabin, the motor chugging away through a dead calm sea, so calm that it was suddenly stopped and the passengers were invited to swim, though there was something about the temperature of the water, warm on the surface with a cold submarine turbulence which brought cramp and headache.

Julia Dickenson said to him, standing by the bow stanchion: You sentimentalise them. They are no more victims than you are to your own alienation. If you had identified with a piece of land, with property and with lineage, you would have had more conviction ... just as they do.

He hadn't been taken seriously.

Julia wore a black costume and dived with that long-legged smoothness and precision, dived clinically, speared over the side like a sailfish. There was something about her that wasn't human. It was attractive, this literalness. It punished him, drove him on. Later he had received a note. It slid under his door and then was given a flick so it became airborne and fluttered at his feet.

If ever you need to talk, I'm a very good listener.

It was from Beatrice Mitchell-Smith.

The storm came in the night. They were out a day from Eddystone Point and were sailing along the top edge of Tasmania, prey to the sudden and erratic storms that lashed the coast. Bass Strait, renowned for its shallowness and ferocity, calm as glass one day and whipping up frightening waves the next, unleashed an unexpected and bilious tempest. The *Nora* made for Stanley. At least, Morris said, there was a smidgen of a breakwater there, at the bottom of a circular curiosity of eroded rock called The Nut. That would do me, Byron Johnson said. The Nut sounded like a good idea. They could make out a brown smudge of land in the spray. The sky grew darker.

Soon it began to rain and everyone went below except Morris and Johnson and the novice at the wheel, and the ones who went below grew violently sick with the fumes and the lack of air since Morris had to run the motor. Suddenly the seas grew heavy, long rolling swells heaving under the ship, and Morris chose to remark he had not seen such seas too often, not even off the Cape, and said it was too late to head for the breakwater, since the wind had changed and the motor couldn't match the current. And so they stood out to sea and were being borne away from the coast at a mighty rate.

Byron Johnson was finally having a real holiday. He clung to the rigging, bellowed at the sea, licked the salt-spray from his arms, allowed the tears to mingle. Finally, finally, he could breathe as though he had developed gills. He sang, and felt the notes melt before him. Captain Morris McGann, peering through cloud and seeing what he thought was a crew member thus engaged in idle and lunatic meditation, ordered Johnson aloft to double-reef the topsail and to furl the foresail. Such a thing was of course rarely heard of at sea. The reputation of losing a passenger was far worse than that of losing a ship. It was the end of any refinancing, for one thing. In any case, Johnson scaled the ratlines ... and a heavy man was he.

The captain was trying to lie under easy sail, as was the rule in a storm, and the barque, being a hermaphrodite, loosed her fore-and-aft mainsail and swung before the wind, rain lashing at the rigging and the ship dipping before the swell. Up on the foremast the sails had parted and a piece of yard-arm had sprung out of the iron. Johnson was trying desperately to embrace the canvas. Up on the crosstrees the world was pitching not only fore and aft but from port to starboard. It was one of those windy ferris rides he might have experienced in Southhampton. His feeble cries calling for the sheets to be pulled taut went unheard above the fury of wind and water.

An eternity went by.

There was, at this time, a strange light which illuminated the horizon. It darted about at first, a metallic phosphor, a 4th of July fuse, and then it drew closer, Byron Johnson becoming transfixed. He tried to reach out for it, one hand trapped between tarry cables, tried to touch its luminescence, to match the nitrous fusion of his body with divine sacrifice, yearning to let go of the responsibility for saving them all. He wanted to visit an obsession; a woman hereabouts, calling from the deep, but heard instead a flat Harvard voice, the tailings of his own imagination and the crackling resonances of Orville Pennington-James:

I do hereby forswear, with my dying pen, such callous nihilism as would allow you to perish forever, the ancient mariner was saying. Allow it upon my head ... manacle me to what happens next! Kid me with curiosity! There is nothing, believe me, on the other side, those voices but beckonings, toings and froings of everyday life. Reality, ha! Accept its regularities; concede its banalities, but upon death there is nothing but words and words hereafter. You've almost said so yourself:

> ... today what characterises our reality is the probability that chaos is the most likely explanation, while at the same time recognising that even to seek an explanation represents a denial of chaos.

Just one more step and you would have had it. Chaos is not worth the effort of nailing reality to the mast. Float, Byron. I've shipped three years before it. Float. I'll furnish thee from mine own library the volumes for thy crossing.

So there Johnson clings, pinned by a lightning bolt ringing the iron 'neath the broken yardarm, brain besieged by the Devil, seduced.

He takes a step. He falls.

The halyards uncoil, slough him off like an albatross loosed from a net and his great wings flap once or twice, too long encaged, too far out to sea, they serve him poorly, and so forlorn, he dives deep into the ocean.

There he was in a kind of calenture, overwhelmed by a desire to be enveloped by the sea. The water was much warmer than he thought, so he believed he was abed, during one of those plunges when people say it is your heart stopping or some such thing, when it is simply the hole of forgetting into which we slip, sometimes for eternity, which serves to remind us that we are never an interruption to anything. Hardly a spark in the great continuum.

He held his breath. When he surfaced, he saw the *Nora*'s running lights sliding away. Then returning. Morris was going through the usual rescue procedure, reconnoitring back and forth over a grid like a dog on a scent. Johnson tried to hold up an arm, but he sank, his arm probably broken when he was ripped from the rigging. Through a lit porthole he saw Julia's husband looking at him. He was practically at eyeball level, but we do not know what possessed the fellow not to raise the alarm. Perhaps it was the play of light and dark. Johnson could see him rubbing his earring. He looked ecstatic. So dark it was, that when a light is on inside, one can see nothing outside. It all depends on the dark, on it being darker, in order to see. Glancing without examining. That is how we love and how we kill. And then he saw Julia rise, push him aside to retch. Saw her lie down again, legs up, the lantern swaying, her feet like alabaster. Perhaps she was lying down all the time, because now Johnson was above the scene on a giant swell, the ship and its jetsam juggling with the line of sight. Julia opened the porthole when the vessel heeled, kicked something into the sea. Closed it again.

The *Nora* disappeared.

Presently Byron Johnson felt something slide beneath his feet. In the strange, purple, celestial light (in this afterburner of the tempest which in future years will be the cause of countless disappearances of vessels ... this I quoth in all sincerity and foreboding), he saw a giant jellyfish, a man-o'-war sneaking up his crotch. The thing was wedging itself there, dear God, ready to sting him athwart the tail. He flailed at it and pulled on it, determined to wrestle any sea monster until the storm had o'erblown. Arrrgh! he shrieked. It was Julia's muslin bloomers. Without much pause for thought, he did what he had been taught at school. (Sailors' trousers ... what d'ye do with sailors' trousers? his teacher had demanded, slipping out of his bell-bottoms.) These were finer. He blew into them and with a deft twist, tied the ends and blew again. Two white sausages gradually appeared. He hitched one final knot and then rested his head in the crotch. Thus he was borne by his own breath through the dark and turbulent sea.

Pennington-James' voice persisted:

At this juncture I was interrupted by a high official from the government, who burst into my hospital room in Hobart, requesting that I, Mr Crusoe, was it? be up and dressed and that I was to report immediately to Government House. He was powdered and hairless and sported no wig. I informed him that I had spent almost two years on a desert isle, that my name was Pennington-James and not Crusoe, nor Robinson, for that matter, and that I was seeking rest, whether eternal or not, a thing entirely between me and Him Upstairs, and would he mind getting his uncontrolled derrière out of my room.

I thought, he blubbered, that you were one of us.

He left this ambiguous statement hanging, patted his braid and minced into the sunlight. It was at that point that I threw the piss-bottle. I was my own man. A life at sea had seen to that.

The next day (there was no warning; these people would interrupt funerals if necessary, disinter corpses, steal heads), two emissaries arrived, made sure I was conscious and then ushered in the Governor himself. His Excellency had thin lips, long sideburns and dandruff and came in humming a hymn. Tall and stooped, he examined me with a monocle which was so thick it appeared that his eye, like God's, encompassed the whole room. I had a faint suspicion I was at the Gates themselves. Everywhere I looked his eye followed until, it seemed, I was swallowed by it. He proceeded with a series of questions, his voice mechanical and toneless. He wanted to know with how many of the native women had I slept. He wanted to know the state of my health and of theirs. He wanted exact calculations of the length of time of their visits. He wanted to know the kinds of food they brought.

I thought he was a most prurient man. But I was generous, contemptuous as I was of his lack of imagination. I was through with writing. Perhaps he could use the material, no doubt published under a *nom de plume*.

He pulled out a gold watch, and with the magnifying glass still in his eye, proceeded to time the interval between my coughing fits. He finally clicked the watch shut, turned abruptly on his heel and exclaimed, it seemed in a moment of passion, *Tremendous!*

The Lieutenant-Governor,
Hobart Town.
Primo December, 1830.

My dear George,

I beg to refer you to Capt. O.J. Pennington-James, late master of the brig Nora (both lying abed, eh what?) for the particulars of the attack the natives made upon the men in Company employ on the 11th December. Capt. Pennington-James was brought from Launceston after his rescue from a lamentable state having been cast away upon an infernal island, and is at present recuperating at Company expense on Northmere.

While the men were collecting cattle along the Great Western Road, they were set upon by natives in a premeditated attack. The blacks made off with several milking beasts. As I mentioned in my last dispatch, some of these natives were captured and dealt with severely. I'm extremely happy to hear that you found that upstart Robinson's report of thirty killed as 'greatly exaggerated'. It was nowhere near that number. Penn-James, however, will not testify, even as he lies upon his deathbed, having also drunk, like Odysseus's comrades, from the milch-cows of the sun-god, and will never return to health.

Yes, milk, dear George. The milk of human kindness. He drank copious amounts of it and all the time grew sicker. This, I beg you to consider, could be the final solution to the native problem, for they do not understand the notion of labour, and we are not about to be ruined for the sake of virtue. The coughing sickness, George, will be far more effective than musket-balls.

I have the honour to be, &c.,
Ed. Curr,
Resident Magistrate,
Tasman Wool Co.
Northmere.

Sperm McGann is standing up in the stirrups of Thomas John's old nag, taking great gulps of fresh air at Circular Head, the freshest air in the world. Didn't want to be like John, lying gangrenous in his hut, did he?

Old John went out and provoked the blacks and copped one in the thigh; thin sliver of a spear with nasty back-raked barbs. No matter how much he broke off, some would remain ... like the blacks. Wonder if they'd poisoned the tips?

Sperm McGann at an easy canter, still standing up in the saddle, shaken with a violent coughing, blood-flecks on his bristly chin, beating at the air with one hand to stay aloft. What a life, these shepherds. They could have easily grazed their sheep and cattle without trouble, but they needed women didn't they? The whole place was short of them. Now they only wanted women with dark fuzzy privates and unashamed offerings and they wanted to pay nothing for the privilege. You always have to give back bigger and better presents. So sheep were taken.

Great draughts of air. That's it. Easy does it. Long

breaths bounced out by the cantering. Will. Health was an act of will. Great gulps of air. Rein in the horse. Arrgh! Look at the sea.

Kicks the horse into a gallop again because up there on the hill his eye catches the movement of black bodies painted into lines ... they think they're menacing that way ... see what a musket will do.

McGann whoops. Turns the old nag which is rearing like a warhorse, leather all white-laced with froth and sweat, the thump of breath and soil. Spurs it back to what was called the 'Race Course'.

When he arrives at the huts he notices first that the smoke from the chimneys is curling to the ground. A shift of wind. He's too exhausted to think too much about it; remembers some vague parable he was forced to learn at the Bosanquets about the smoke from sacrifices ... God's dissatisfaction.

But he forgot that on a shift of wind the natives come, downwind, but the white men wouldn't smell them anyway, mouths stuffed full of fatty mutton and beer.

McGann can hardly breathe. Dismounts when the outlying dogs bark. Receives the first spear before he can turn around. It's surprising at first, this quivering rod stuck in the side of his chest. Then a fiery pain and he falls, more from comprehension and shock, and sees the blacks scooting through the tea-tree, maybe twenty of them, suddenly his collapsed lung bringing massive relief despite the pain, and he can breathe once more, his hand at his side warmed with blood. He shifts into a sitting position, places his other hand around the wound and pulls the shaft, then sucks at his fingers full of blood and soil and crawls inside towards a fire, plunges into its redness and feels it sear the wound and he coughs once and sees his insides spewing out, hears the hollowness in his ear, waves of fainting. Bloody nonsense, he says. All bloody fear. He thinks he's talking, but hasn't said a word in reality. Looks around him and sees stinking boots and vomit and piss and blood.

G'day, Sperm. Whatcha do? Fall off yer horse?

Thomas John is lying on the floor, breathing his last, three spears in his back.

III

Amongst Those Left Are You …

— it would be just like your sort to go so far as to invite reader participation in the remaining two volumes of the trilogy!

B.S. Johnson
See The Old Lady Decently

He wrote that a few months before committing suicide, the first in his Matrix Trilogy, which he never completed. He left that to me. The ancient Greeks had a word for it: *tessera*. A piece of broken tile which completed a puzzle.

My name is Thomas McGann. And I want to know why he committed suicide.

Even now, when I read his work, it is as though he is holding it open for me. He must have begun the second volume at about the time my stepmother bought an old run-down motel in Queenstown on the west coast of Tasmania. It consisted of cabins, a dozen of them running haphazardly along the highway, old miners' shacks built on piers, converted into tolerable accommodation. The slagheaps in the background loomed, cast into landmarks on the neon motel sign in a vain attempt to pick up some of the passing tourist trade. Almost nobody stopped.

Nobody of note.

It rained a lot, and in the winter, a constant sleeting. The motel was constructed of Huon pine. It was waterproof. But there were no trees anywhere to be seen. A mining town like a moonscape. In between stripping beds and shaking out sticky condoms, cleaning up vomit, vacuuming the carpets and flipping eggs 'easy over' in the mornings, I began writing the last part of Johnson's trilogy, sitting at the registration desk in the middle of the night and listening for the change of gears which suggested custom. It was a kind of memorial, I suppose, though it was questionable for whom it was intended. Perhaps I was calling him down, pleading for a guiding hand to show a stutterer on his way; or perhaps even as a guide, his Virgilian shyness and distemper may have matched the complicities of my ancestors. Although ... come to think of it ... there was a salt-encrusted hand, barnacled with age and tutored in perversity which strove hard in the telling to hold things together. Deadly enemies, truth and fiction. It's a crisis in every age.

Reception was in a new bungalow built on a slab. The former owners didn't heed engineering principles. Every time it rained, water rushed down the hills, collected the slag and flooded us with black ink. A pump switched on automatically, sluiced the stuff into a downpipe. I can still hear it, or is that my heart? There it goes. Over it and behind the thin partition, the snores of my stepmother. Times like these my mind invariably drifted between tenses.

Though I'd outlasted B.S.Johnson (on the mainland, my average life span would be just about up), I had nothing in common with him except perhaps a dead mother. Although I was looking for truth as hard as he did, all I was uncovering were lies about my own life.

Meanwhile my stepmother kept me enslaved in the motel with illnesses she'd invented while I laboured and she counted money, complaining of cancer. I don't doubt her anxiety about death. I won't cry at her funeral either, unless the moment overtakes me. I ladle out porridge from the aluminium saucepan, its handle burning my hand. I can ill afford that. My stepmother pulls her beanie down over her eyes. It's three degrees in the kitchen. Food stains mark the walls. Between the chopping board and the greasy toaster, there is a hole in the wall made by mice. That's where she keeps her money. I put my hand in, feel the softness of a rat; push the money-belt down my shirt.

Down the road, at Macquarie Harbour, they endured much more for a lesser crime a hundred and fifty years ago: deathly cold, poor food, disease, torture, the worst excesses of human nature. There was no escaping Sarah Island; neither by sea nor through the impenetrable wilderness, and it was easy to be spotted from observation posts which were watched as well by others from their own hiding places and peepholes, others who didn't mind the cold and so stood unmoving, sleet melting off their greased hair, watching the fires and the drunkenness and the sweaty clasp of man upon man in the loneliest winters of the cruelest station.

Then there was a girl looking like Lady Diana. She arrived late one night in a dented taxi, smoking a lot of cigarettes and making a dozen phone-calls and all the while I was hoping the secretiveness I admired in her wouldn't turn out to be something vulgar. So that was all I had to go on. Oh, and a copy of *Albert Angelo,* signed by B.S.J. himself. It wasn't available in Australia because H.M.Customs had seized the whole consignment since the text included holes cut in the pages and they wanted to view the offending excisions. The book smelled like someone had smoked a hundred cigarettes in it, the sixties hermetically sealed in print. I wrote to the bookseller in Hammersmith, who wrote back that, yes, I could have one smelling of Guinness if I liked, at £200. I wasn't the only B.S.J. collector. At least the girl wasn't going to charge for her story, even if I was too shy to talk to her. Later I plucked up the courage, went to her room with a bottle of milk and showed her my copy, annotated, the margins filled with sequel, the blank pages scored with scribble. I grew dizzy then, and had to sit on the edge of her bed.

In Tasmania, the best minds of my generation were failing the heritage test, for we were half-castes, destined to be hated by all; not of one mind; caught, as they say, between the devil and the deep blue sea; patronised by some and regarded as curiosities by others. Don't be fooled by my white hair and pink eyes. I'm an albino. Not at all the same as those who have been worshipped here for well on a century: the large, the grey and the muttony. We had our own myths, and depending on the occasion, could turn them and turn them again, possessing a talent for the international stage, whose roving spotlight would soon find its mark.

The girl gave no name, but placed a cross where she had to sign. She had travelled most of the night from Cape Grim in the north-west corner of Tasmania and there was much desperation in her. I watched her come out of her cabin at two in the morning and walk barefoot to the phone-box by the main road. She was in there for exactly thirty-six minutes.

I could well have imagined what had happened at Cape Grim; the massacres, the violation of our mothers, the shoals of execrating silence. But what possessed her was far worse than history. I wasn't prepared for that. Wasn't prepared for it to be so close; for until that time my hand had been unsteady ... and well ... when it came to the pen, one hoary hand was as good as another.

When it came to the knife as well. Even though I'm studying medicine, they'll never let me practise; not even as a G.P. Not with this stump of an arm, out of which grows a finger; a fully-formed finger, mind you, capable of grotesqueries. Imagine telling a patient to relax while I stick it up his bum, or grasping a scalpel with it to incise, excise, circumcise, exorcise whatever. No. There was no equal opportunity in this profession, which grew from humble and despised origins ... I mean the clinical side of it: butchering, barbering, vivisection, crusading wars. In those days a stump would not have been despised. Let the deformed dissect the putrefying. It was licence for the ignoble. To them fell prosaic anatomy. Real doctors dealt only with poetry of the spirit. And what a mess they made, philosophers and critics.

Enough. I wear a long knitted glove over the stump and try to look like a pop star. For a long time they wouldn't let me join a golf club down in Hobart. Though I think that was for a different reason. I learned to agitate, but I'm mostly seen with pity. Most folks still think I eat a muesli of white ants for breakfast; maybe suck opium out of a didgeridoo high on a one-note samba. No, hang on a minute, we're not Asian. I play upon it when it suits. Sell an odd bark painting or two executed with execrable pointillism which, when seen from afar resembles the face of Dali. I prefer jokes at other's expense, but always end up paying. It's written on the body: I can count my friends on one hand. I wouldn't lift a finger. Etc. But you could say I've made the most of my disability. It opened doors. I have a knob on the steering wheel of my Volkswagen which helps me to drive with one hand. And when it comes to the crunch you'd be surprised how strong the finger could be.

Let's see. I've got thirty-six minutes.

See that?

Penguin.

Nah, too white.

Albino seal, matey. Chucked out of the tribe.

There it is again.

Could be King Penguin. Curious little bastards. Walk right up to be killed.

Down Macquarie Island they put 'em in digesters. Four thousand a day. Boiled 'em alive for oil.

Whitey's way, eh. The commodification of nature. No fuckin' respect.

There, look.

Sea-cow, I reckon.

An empty expanse of ocean. Black water and spindrift and a jagged surface; but deep below, listen to the squealings of submarine play, Cetacean delight, all having a whale of a time as the pod tosses him like a football upon their spouting heads, scoring his back to bring him shoreward with barnacled intelligence.

Thinking he was already dead, Byron Johnson felt the floor of heaven beneath his feet. He was careful not to take a false step. It felt like a dance-hall, smoothly waxed parquetry. Shuffle shuffle, cha-cha-cha. Ainslie jigging up close to him, her breasts ebbing and flowing, legs electric in the strobe near the juke-box in Stromboli's Café. Slip. Slide. Turn her around. The floor moves. Broken beer glass. Slip-slide on his back.

Jonah Johnson is vomited up on shore and dumped onto sand. The recoiling wave wrenches him back a little. His stomach heaves, he floats. This is a joke, he thinks. It's necessary to make a joke of everything at sea. Figures moving on the shoreline. Soon he is hauled up. They wrap him in a blanket, give him a sip of brandy. Worse thing you can do to a drowned man. Soon there's a fire inside and out. He retches.

Who are you?

Birders.

Berbers? Am I in Africa? Must've been treading water a long time.

You're on an island, matey.

I ...aaagh!

He sank into unconsciousness and awoke periodically, but had lost the ability to speak.

You watch them, these birders. Some white, some dark. They speak little and move slowly. Hundreds of campsites along the beach, fires flaring and smoke hanging blue beneath the cliff face. They speak only of the 'season'. They glide, dark shapes in feathers and boots. They ask no questions, but give you clothes and food and shelter. You want to say you've fallen off a ship, but they shake their heads. You tell them you're a writer, but they shake their heads and laugh, showing very white teeth. You ask them where you are and they say you're on an island. That is all you know. Mostly these people just shake their heads. Perhaps because you cannot form a basic sentence; with a verb, a subject and an object. Amen. It is a great relief. Example:

How?

How? Are you a native American?

How get here?

Ah! You must've drifted off a boat.

See?

See what?

You.

We are Aborigines. So the anthropologists insist. We come for muttonbird, every March for five weeks. We come for *Yolla. Yolla* is a short-tailed shearwater full of fat and oil. *Puffinus tenuirostris.* They have strong wings and fly thousands of miles a year. When the blackwood blossoms, they arrive here and build burrows in the sandy soil. Come. I'll show you. See this one here? Put your hand in.

Nnnngh.

Go on, grab him by the beak.

Furry.

Yeah. Break his neck. Like this.

She held the bird in her hand like a tiny dead Cupid. She was the most beautiful woman he had ever seen, but she killed cherubim and in doing so, brought him back to life.

Your name?

Emma.

Kidding.

No. She smiled. Oh, God, the sadness of that smile!

Her name was Emma. Emma McGann, and the whales had brought him to her. She wasn't surprised. She said she knew he was coming. Her brother Tom told her she could make things happen simply by writing.

His heart was pounding. Just the sight of that thin, willowy girl striding up from the beach with plastic buckets of seawater was enough to make him faint. Her feet in sandals. Ankles wrought by the gods of Egypt. Hair a veil of lapis lazuli. Had trouble speaking though. Pity. Yes, sometimes she was incomprehensible and sometimes she completed his sentences. But on the whole it became a wordless love, a labour of lockjaw. Upon their meeting, nothing was more desirable.

Nights there would be fires, seen and transcribed from one island to the next. They appeared out of the past, hair matted, wearing kangaroo skins, sunburnt, healthy and wild-eyed, their huts in twos and threes along the coastal fringes. In the sheds, the women still working into the night by oil-lamps, heads in shower caps all covered with feathers, scalding, brushing and laying the muttonbirds on racks; washing, grading, sprinkling them with salt and packing them into barrels for New Zealand; pouring in brine and watching for the spud to float up when the salt was right.

Maybe she'd chosen him to be the potato, he thought. A gauge of some kind. A prater; maybe a prat.

She heard voices, she said. He did too when he began to work in the sheds, plucking and brushing alongside her, long days and long hours of dirty work accompanied by a howling radio. Huge draughts of steam caulked with humid down clogged his lungs, filtered through his teeth and choked him when he opened his mouth. Feathers rained into his hair, bird oil shot like sperm into his face. It took a week for him to do it properly. Even then, the birds he processed were always smaller than the rest. Emma said if he worked faster he'd get the bigger ones. She would smile at him and his heart would melt. When he went to his bunk at night he slept in the feathers of a million birds, his dreams borne by an unending flight of petrels, Emma somewhere there, in the light of desire. But there was always the noxious consequence of realising he had been unable to give himself to the sea. Human, all too human.

He knocked on her door. Men's quarters over th'other way, one of the women indicated with a disapproving chin. But Emma dragged him into her room, holding his wrist lightly, and made him tea. She wore a long tee-shirt bordered with a colourful motif. It was the same, he noticed, as the border around her letter-paper and envelopes. Later, she led him out the back, into an old truck, and drove him steadily and competently up onto a dirt road. In the moonlight he watched her manoeuvring the wheel with one hand, imagined her breasts beneath the tee-shirt. He dozed and woke and dozed again with the rhythm. He was unborn and she had no substance and he felt the most curiously unfocussed desire. She was beautiful, truly beautiful. So beautiful that he was soon passing out, in and out, images of his life reeling from A to Z and back again. She made a fire, heated a can of soup and fed him from it.

A weak sun creased the horizon. When he woke he was wet and cold and lying on a cliff ledge. He couldn't move. Suddenly the air was beaten, feathers flew and when he looked up he saw a helicopter hovering there, basket spiralling out like a spider scurrying to check for movement and soon two men appeared, wrapped him up in foil like a fish finger and took him off the island under protest, strapped into a papoose.

Author rescued from sea

Byron Johnson, avongard British author was yesterday rescued from a rocky ledge after having fallen off a boat and spending some time in the water. Mr Johnson, suffering from hyperhernia and hallucinations, told the *Northwestern News* he was saved by a pod of whales and a million muttonbirds. Sgt Bryce of the Stanley constabulary said that this was quite common.

Well, thirty-six minutes or my name isn't Thomas McGann.

When the girl came out of the phone-box I knew I would have to talk to her, tell her I'd discovered a writer called B.S. Johnson who wrote about us Tasmanians.

And that was how I met Ainslie Cracklewood some years back when she had run out of money in the Apple Isle.

Johnson? she frowned. He's my husband.

It was raining lightly, but even then the motor began, thumping and throbbing and sluicing black water. It was a sound which connected, gave me an uncontrollable desire to be linked with genius, and when later I'd brought books and a bottle of milk to her room, that shabby room noisy as a drum, she'd already seduced me, long before she had touched my stump and had discovered absence made for twice the excitement and even longer before my own discovery of her obsession with disability.

You don't get a girl like that often. I mean, who allowed perversity to get the better of pity. Maybe it was just my style, the way I wrenched at the steering wheel of my VW, the way I avoided disabled parking spaces, the way I spat through the little side window. I simply didn't care. We drove up to the Cape, rippling buttongrass brown as onion soup, the car percolating from lookout to lookout, and we necked and kissed until our lips were paralysed. We went down the coast and stayed in the best hotels while it rained constantly. We spent two nights at the Sheraton with a harbour view on my stepmother's money and watched the glitter on the waterfront, though Ainslie didn't come near the window and wouldn't let me turn on the lights. She said her father would be sending someone after her if she wired home for money. She slept on the spare bed. I liked that kind of paranoia. It made her dependent. For a powerful woman, she had vulnerability. She showed it in the most delicate emotional striptease. I was ready to follow her back to London.

It didn't work out as planned, of course. It was almost a year later before I got my grant to go, and in the meantime my stepmother had died. She wasn't joking, she said. My stepmother's last words. I carry them engraved upon my heart.

When I arrived in London I didn't bother looking Ainslie up for a few weeks. She would keep. No good scurrying for the safe and familiar in my business. That's why they picked me to collect WORÉ's remains from the British Museum.

Who were they?

They were my people. We were very closely knit. After one genocide you didn't branch out much.

There were three children. When our real mother died the extended family looked after us. When they died, we were fostered out. Emma and I were twins. And then there was Jimmy. Jimmy was born with a bubble on the back of his head which went pink and yellow, and when it was cold, blue. Then they amputated the bubble and Jimmy's head was covered in blood and Mum said the spinal fluid wasn't going to form there anymore. Jimmy grew up listless and silent and it was a long time before he could speak. When he did speak there were long silences. Slowed down by his disability, he always seemed to have time, like a great footballer with a clearing kick, appearing ridiculous to some and profound to others. But life was cruel and things changed rapidly.

Jimmy began knocking off car badges, turning them into belt buckles and selling them to other kids, and while I was watching him one day two policemen nabbed us, one with his arm around Jimmy's neck and one holding my stump up my back. At the station I convinced them Jimmy was a retard and even undid his shirt to show the scars on the back of his neck and said how the spinal fluid would run if the skin was punctured and if this yellowy stuff came out it would mean he would die in their custody, particularly since they were manhandling him, their big police paws slapping at him, since Jimmy was falling off to sleep. He did that often when there was stress. They'd never dealt with disability before, so they let us go with a caution and said we were lucky not to cop a size 12 police boot, to boot. I knew then that I had a gift. Knew that I had to speak. For Jimmy; for all the contradictions. Maybe it was because I had the sun and the sea and I knew there was something there beyond thought, in the same way that Jimmy was beyond misery.

Then, a week later, Mum died of a heart attack. Jimmy went to sleep in Uncle Ronnie's car and Uncle Ronnie went fishing and left the car in gear because the handbrake didn't work and somehow the car jumped into gear on the slope and went walloping down over the rocks and settled very slowly into the water, hardly making a sound. When Uncle Ronnie came back the car was gone, and he cursed and swore and wondered why he'd ever taught the kid to drive.

It was then that I began to agitate. I've been agitating ever since. And that was how I got to London.

Not through agitation. I'd written a book. But I did have a particular voice that was hard to ignore. I used to go to every demonstration, proclaim with passion my own private repression. It embarrassed people. Passion always did. They tried hard to connect with it. And when politicians attended, I could wheel out a three-pronged irony which made them uneasy. People loved cripples. They partly identified, partly felt guilty, partly respected its power ... all of which could be reversed at any moment. People were parts. My gift lay in that recognition. I revelled in complication, ambivalence, ambiguity. I could cross the floor at any time, convinced the most indecent operation of the human mind was the either/or, or the bifurcated brain. That's why I could speak outside of logic, of that dark irrationality forbidden to moralists, of that deeper purpose: graceful and transcendent malignancy.

That's why I was deputised to collect WORÉ's head from the British Museum.

The curator had no idea I was coming. What's the name? he asked, shuffling along germ-ridden backrooms amongst the mummies. I told him we didn't name the dead ... WORÉ simply meant woman. Oh, we have heaps of tribal cadavers, he said.

The authorities were accommodating ... a traditional strain of politeness practised towards madmen and savages who came to claim. They rolled out the red carpet for Ghandi, but gave me scones and tea instead, relieved this wasn't the Elgin Marbles all over again and I did some signing, even an autograph here and there. Then they brought out a cardboard box and I ceremoniously wrapped it with a flag I'd brought with me and transported it slung from a shoulder strap from Russell Square to my digs in Clapham, on the Tube and all the way felt someone watching me, watching over the relics.

Don't get me wrong. I felt entrusted with a sacred duty; but you had to see the parts that weren't so sublime: having my great-great-grandmother's head in a box under my bed in a cold B & B in East Clapham. Nights I read medical books. Kept up with my studies.

> **Autophony:** a form of auscultation in which the examiner speaks close to the patient's chest and notes the modification in his own voice as affected by the conditions of the patient's chest.

Back home the newspapers unkindly said I was listening to the Community Chest, but mainly I was listening to my own ... oh, the feelings that cannot be articulated there! The sensitivities which would render me powerless after a century and a half of pent-up frustration. Yet I dreaded the emptiness underneath it all ... the inaccessible self. No such thing as an individual. We are the sum of our ideas. Mamamamamamama. Quaquaquaquaquaqua. In the dead of night I spoke, with my ear to the box, my hand which they had shaken and betrayed when alive and black, on my beating heart.

A week later, when I had almost run out of money, my publishers rang to say I was on the shortlist for a prize. I demanded an upgrade. So they put me in a five-star hotel in Knightsbridge and I went to call on Ainslie.

Ainslie Cracklewood. When I saw her again in London she was more desirable than ever. Gone was the tourist, the unsettled, restless traveller, the seeker after experience. Here she was displaying the vulnerability, danger and lethargy of one who has recently shed a husband. Yes, you could say a slow reptilian fire burned in her, a passionate and smouldering intensity waxing and waning with the day, a consumption devoutly to be avoided. I went up in the lift with my box. I took it everywhere since hotel staff could not be trusted.

Ainslie's apartment was a huge space, a kind of penthouse in Bloomsbury, with attic windows and slate clattering down into the guttering when I shook open the windows. It was unnaturally warm. I had a desire to sprint across the floor, from the door to the front windows. It was long enough for a good sprint, but stopping would have been difficult, especially with the window open. I come from a long line of jumpers. Ainslie, I could see, wasn't in the mood for such activity.

I can't even conceive of sprinting now. It's become just another word, when once it signalled inspiration. A muse, a sprite. Blythe once, it now hobbles in a walking frame and I take advantage, pummelling it for ideas. Memory cannot recuperate the feeling of love. No one wants to recall murder either. There would be a moment when I tried to push the muse over a cliff. But more of that later ...

Ainslie wore a short, black silk skirt and a black sweater. It was the fashion then. She tottered and swooned when she opened the door and I had to catch her to stop her from hitting the floor, then she staggered to a hammock in the middle of the room tied to two Tasmanian Blackbutt trunks set between floor and ceiling, and she lay down, mildly swinging, the back of a hand on her forehead. I had forgotten how beautiful her legs were, awkwardly straddling the webbing, trapped in this childish and obscene pose like a tiny nymph in a wicked spindle.

Finally. You've finally come.

Ainslie loved drama.

Not yet. I still had the box in my arms. That was the moment when I wanted to sprint, all the way to the window, toss out the box and my sacred duty and fall upon the hammock in awkward compromise. But I made her a drink and we talked instead about the good times in Tasmania and about how I took my stepmother's money and we lived it up in swank hotels and how she'd never really wanted to sleep with me, even though we made love in cars, lifts, cinemas, at the back of a coach. No, Ainslie always slept alone. Come to think of it, I can't even imagine the hammock now. It was impossible for two, I was thinking as I stood in her flat, thinking how desperate she was to be alone. Later, of course, she told me.

So, as she swung there grieving, she told me that her ex-husband Byron Johnson, the writer, was in the next apartment and that if I opened the door a little it would enthral him ... do you see that little peephole, the spyhole with the bird's eye view? You'll see a shadow fall across it now.

She sipped her drink.

I left the door slightly ajar.

It helps his writing, she said wistfully, stirring her brandy with her little finger and sucking it, not particularly daintily.

There was a cold breeze coming through the open window carrying smells of the city: car fumes, sewer and fish-shop exhaust. This high up and the air was still bad. It was trying to snow, but the clouds were choking.

It is almost the late twentieth century, Ainslie said, and he is still thinking he may be becoming someone else in writing. He fears overturning his faith in integrity, virtue, honesty and all that workingman nonsense. He fears voices. He fears words which can be manipulated, deconstructed. You know what he told me the other day? He said suicide was the ultimate imagination. Did this mean he believed in it or not?

She sighed and sucked.

Really, she continued with her hand between her legs, bunching up her silk skirt so that it flowered over her other hand which was holding the glass, he's afraid of becoming unhinged from his central self. Messy isn't it? All men are the same, she said, no multiple utterances, only the lonely gasp of the heady Central Committee.

I didn't know what to think. Did she dress up like this and invite men in so Byron could write, or was it so she could mock him? Perform some sort of matinée, a porno peepshow to satisfy an ancient sadistic passion of her own? I went into one of the other rooms, placed the box on a solid teak cabinet and sat down on a chair. I rattled the box. Nothing shook. Removed the flag.

I was going to open the box when Ainslie came in. She undressed. She took the flag. Draped it around herself. I suppose it was that gesture more than anything which sowed the seed of doubt. Her grand movement, replete with sex and death ... yes, I imagined Ainslie would die in a plane crash over a South American jungle and they would bring her body out draped in the same way, perhaps in different colours ... so much was possible ... her swirling set my mind ablaze with equivocation. The flag was my toga and I felt like Nero, who didn't start the fire that destroyed Rome, but who picked up on the cheap real estate afterwards. There were abundant analogies and I grew tired of the commonality, for it was a decisive, naked and lonely moment and I hung onto it like the last man on an island, my sensitivities bared, though there was no one to see.

What did I stand for? Was it for mankind which had invented itself through the defects of a positive classification and which would soon disappear into other, more refined systems? I longed for the unwritten, for the impossibility to write ... I longed for the last gasp of a death which would release me from the constant extinction of myself. Perhaps I longed for Jimmy's death, knowing I was not big enough, knowing my heart didn't have the capacity to understand the unity of death, to understand the tightening form, or formalism, of a freedom in retreat from the systems trying to rescue it. Yes, progress was an eternal spiral down or up ... it had no direction.

My anguish was a soft fall into the quiet recesses of the heart. There I found truth could be entrancing and treacherous. I noticed that the peephole was dark.

Anyway, all this took up much energy, so it was little wonder I didn't know at the time that Ainslie had a hidden agenda. I should have suspected it, when later her friends arrived. They were mainly women, though there was a Lord _____, who wore a monocle which he fiddled with a lot so I suspected it was a prop, and later suspected even more when he returned from the bathroom with his jacket undone and I glimpsed a slim waist, and what's more, an impressive *Pectoralis major.* I asked if he lifted weights. Gosh no, s/he said. I should have suspected. It was the way they kissed each other, the way they wanted to build houses in rainforests, to strike out into the wilderness, to establish Amazonian sovereignty where felons had feared to tread. I should have realised this was where Ainslie was retreating. But for the moment she was also equivocal, so we struck an accord.

She said she was Sapphic, maybe not quite; not entirely.

It's okay, I replied. Your verse is fine. I'm black, but maybe not quite; not entirely ... and that's much worse.

No matter how bad, the Overseas Trip is always a good memory. I remember with happiness London's stink, the slush in the streets, the uncollected garbage, musty hotels and the pheromones of certain women. Otherwise, it had been a devastating winter.

Back in Tasmania there was nothing but fresh air, health, nature, beauty writ large. It was painful for a while in Hobart. Then one day I heard the wind come. An icy rain followed and suddenly the season had changed. The streets were littered with leaves, piled thickly and stickily along the paths. I watched the boats tie up smugly beside each other, saw the water crease and then whip as the wind changed and when I looked up, Mount Wellington was covered in snow.

I abandoned my studies, took groups of Americans up the West Coast in a bus (read B.S. Johnson while driving) and unloaded them in Queenstown at my stepmother's motel. George, her partner, owned it now. He didn't mention giving me a cut. He watched every move I made, counted the cutlery in the dining-room twice. Sometimes my sister came for rides in the coach, sitting up the back writing things on tiny slips of paper. I took the Americans to the coast, to the wilderness, to the rainforests. Some of them were so old I expected them to die. They carried very heavy packs. They panted and puffed, but they kept going on pills and nerves. They took the beautiful emptiness with them back to the subways of New York, to the slaughterhouses of Chicago, to the freeways of L.A. They unpacked it for their friends and found it curiously ... debilitating. After a while they will say it didn't do much for them. Next year they'll go to the Grand Canyon and get drunk instead.

Back in Tasmania my people buried WORÉ's head in a sacred site. Nobody thought to unwrap it or to get it X-rayed. There was a scuffle when we banned TV cameras and the press said we were wrong-headed.

Back in Tasmania Ainslie and I rented a run-down house at Sisters' Beach with a bay frontage, a view of a small island and children shitting in the shallows. And had our first row. Coincidentally a storm blew up. It seemed to take the force out of the quarrel, but something lingered: a hardness impossible to soak through; the impermeable nature of the day-to-day. It was a deferred existence and so hardened were we that it would have surprised us to see how worm-eaten we were already, porous with grief.

You are, Ainslie screamed, exhibiting the same bloody deplorable characteristics!

She let this accusation hang. She had got rid of other men in the same way. She meant, of course, my ambivalence; my lack of will to act. She meant my ancestry. Even Wally Arthur, who was the first to send petitions to the British Government, whom she'd dug up and traced as one of my great great grand-uncles, was nothing but a drunken paranoid fence-sitter infected with Christianity. So she said. Maybe her research was going badly. She went on shouting. Her eyes were furious. She must've had a P.A. system implanted in her throat. Her voice carried across the water and circled the island. People gathered by the front fence. They heard her from as far away as the corner shop. The next day they gave me suspicious looks as I carried the bread home under my crippled arm.

We moved further up the coast. Ainslie wanted to build a house in the bush. It was a sign of her insecurity, perhaps of the raw chip she carried on her shoulder about not having had a formal education (though I said this never really helped anyone), her fury at not having had the time, flying around to polo matches instead of putting in a couple of good, solid years on Jane Austen. Her friends, who came to visit and help, were women with PhDs who spoke in strange accents, went to conferences in Cuba and rode motorcycles. I was attracted to more than a few, but they kept out of my way. They were handy with building materials.

Ainslie and I quarrelled more often and whenever that happened, I always went for an extended walk alone. Sometimes I lit fires and watched the grass burn and the weeds redden like melting wire and thought how they used to fire the grasses, the flames inducing a trance, the animals on the move and then the wild and terrible excitement of the hunt. You could smell it still, in the air. Sometimes the fire got away.

When I read in the papers that Byron Johnson had been washed up nearby, I rang my sister Emma and told her that her letters had finally been answered. Because Ainslie never read the papers, because Ainslie never read anything much, I didn't bother to tell her.

I used to be in the motel business. Only thing is, it was such a long time ago ... the damp walls, the squeaky beds, the porridge in the mornings. Gaol's like a motel for you, they said.

So full of rage it's difficult to talk.

Yes, in and out of institutions. One, I remember, on a hill surrounded by pines. The daily decisions: whether to self-mutilate or not. See these scars. People used to think they were tribal markings when I demonstrated, bare-chested on the barricades. Each day an inscription, or else a generous dose of mind-numbing drugs. Each day a litany of afflictions, the groans, the mental sluicing, the unwillingness to love, to live, the tears which will not come, and then suddenly, the mysterious appearance of hurt and anger which went too deep. My emotions were manufactured for war. But in the homes they numbed them, made a space for silent observation. They taught me to be clinical. Yes, the silence killed, and I wrote about it, about the boring progression of alcoholism, dementia, paranoia, attachment to the House Mother, weaning, alienation, signing myself out by holding a knife to her throat on staff payday. Went to live with my stepmother in a motel and then shacked up with an Englishwoman who nursed me back to health. That last a bit of a fairy-tale. But Ainslie Cracklewood did have connections and money, and I had a book written and the rest is pretty much as I have detailed it.

Well, I took the long walk back.

In memory, I mean, when in reality I was walking along the beach and saw the building on the hill which once housed me, turned ironically into a hotel. I walked up onto the road.

There was a Four Square store making the most of its Coke sign. This was the boondocks: logging trucks careering down the hill; a few shacks and ringbarked stands of blackwood; cows stringing out, coming for hay unfurled from an old Texas police car, its star painted on haphazardly; the hotel looking like a blockhouse presiding over middens of shells, unmarked Aboriginal sites, piles of quarried rock filling a lunar landscape studded with tea-tree and silver banksia dwarfed by wind; there were warm salt pools and beyond that the wild and roaring sea driving driftwood dense and dark as nightwrecks up onto the foundations of a demolished lighthouse. The thistles have gone, the spoors are dead, the rye grass grows yellow and pale and waves in the cold wind. On the horizon busy forklifts shuttled to and fro in a timberyard whose sign said: *Safety Record: 12 days.*

'The Bass Strait Jacques' was the rather grand title of a run-down guesthouse ... in keeping with exotic French names around this coast and the low-brow tourists who didn't mind crud. It was billed as a family hotel, which meant kids could go into the beer garden. The kids looked pretty nasty. I walked in. The 'Star Wars Bar'. Neon spangles shooting up into the ceiling. Shotguns on the wall and a big sticker that said ARMY BRINGS OUT THE BEST IN YOU, next to an old cat skin under which someone had written: PAT PUSSY, BUT NO FREE DRINKS. Didn't think I could drink there anyway. But then drinking's my problem and that's another story. The locals called it the B.S. Jakes, though that sounded like a urinal on a leaky boat and that's what it really was. The spa water was suspiciously yellow. I noticed they hadn't fixed the gutters and the wind was still causing the downpipes to bang like demented wind chimes. I knew that sound like others knew tunes they couldn't erase. It used to do bad things to me.

I went out the back. Once a gas bottle exploded near the kitchens and the remains of two dogs carpeted the lawns for a considerable distance. I walked past the other wing, loosening memories ... of an orphan amongst others, of the drizzling sky and tensed bladders held against draconian discipline, of crude intercourse with laundry maids, of herpes and fights and old cicatrices like mystic inscriptions on the skin of the dead. It was a kind of pride by which you could live. My arm was an added distinction. Curious dogs came to be stroked by it, wedging up beside me for the exceptional finger behind the ear.

Here it is. Used to be the old shower block. Steam and shit-encrusted windows, broken louvres we once used for weapons, slinging them like boomerangs standing only thirty feet apart, nicked with splintering glass if we were lucky, bleeding into toilet bowls after frenzied punch-ups, an inferno of sound and smell and pain.

They've turned it into a gymnasium. Fat men trying to lift weights now, toning up for the summer season. The spa spews steam. The naked and hairy waddle and flap in awkward thongs, in and out of the pool like giant turtles. Against the fogged-up glass, children are giggling.

Boong! Coon! they yell.

A black man dismounts from the stationary cycle, limps slowly to the spa.

Go back to Africa!

I walk up to the kids. Fuck off. I hit one over the ear.

They stroll away. Don't worry about him, one says to another.

They can't find an insult for one so white. Kids are always a great comfort to each other.

I look through the glass. He looks very like the writer Salman Rushdie. I go in. At the desk, which nobody is tending, I slide my finger down the register. I'm wrong. No such name. Of course, I say to myself, he's incognito.

I strip to my shorts. Step into the spa with him. He shifts to make room. His thinning hair and hooded eyes are unmistakable. We nod to each other.

A really good idea, I say.

What? he asks.

Tasmania.

Yes.

We splash around a little. He is observing me suspiciously. I change tack.

Are you on holidays? On a tour? I run charters.

Shipwrecked.

Oh. I knew the answer. I'd been shipwrecked many times before. I hold out a friendly hand. He had a nervous tic, an over-expressive face in a silent movie.

The name's McGann.

He knew.

You've heard of me?

Everyone's a McGann around here, he says.

There aren't *that* many. I do a ball-park estimate of maybe a couple of hundred, including all the cousins that aren't cousins, related through cohabitation and proximity and fellow feeling and ancient kinships, tribal loyalties, reinventions, deep-song structures. I register a complaint. This was a sweeping statement.

The truth, he says ... submerging and then surfacing after a full five minutes during which I've ordered a couple of double daiquiris from the Star Wars Bar ... is only anxiety over a belief in truth.

I was hoping the drink would make him less enigmatic, expecting a world-famous author to be almost prolix.

When we speak, we are all McGanns, he says.

He lifts his forearm from the water and places it side by side against my stump.

We're not related are we? I ask. You never know.

Amnesia, he says ... collective amnesia makes us all guilty, each to each ... guilty relations.

Some others joined us in the spa and since this wasn't ancient Greece the philosophy was embarrassing, so I suggested we towel down and drink some more in the beer garden.

He came here to die, he said, after his second whisky for which I had paid an above average price. And then he detailed my family history. To my astonishment, he mentioned the name.

Yes, he said, Sperm rid himself of tuberculosis through obsession alone, riding these cliff-tops every morning.

He gulped down his drink and then, seeing mine, swallowed that too. Strange for a Pakistani caught on the wrong side of Partition.

Come, he said. I'll show you.

I followed. It was the sort of thing you did with mentors. We walked along a line of pines towards the creek. There was a wind. He stumbled once or twice over fallen branches and pine cones and I had to support him with my good arm as we walked over the wooden bridge. Under it, the stained water rippled red and frothy. We climbed the hill on the other side, following a sheep track, trying at first not to step on the pellets and then, resigned to the amount, tramped over them. Presently the trees ended, the stunted bushes thinned and a heath extended along the hilltop, tussocky grass concealing the steepness of the cliff-edge. At the top, he pointed to a clearing.

There! he shouted and strode off.

Here, he said, panting, this is where he would have come. Here, kneel. Our age forbids such intimacy. Kneel, for God's sake and listen to the hacking cough, the dry fever of an afternoon drawn to the coolness of an open door; out there the sea beyond the hut, here, the remains of a chimney crumbling to a husk, still black these stones, plates of simple clay he held heated to his chest, and there engraved with the image of his lungs, fragments of mottling and cavitation; here, feel the wind and its time entering through the stone where the lintel and threshold have fused, just there he would have stood, contemplating the opening, as if the afternoon had let him down, rejected his plea for the next rising of the sun; listen; smell the salt upon that sea and you can smell him, the clothes on him all he had, maybe a bedroll and a quartpot or two flapping and clanging about him and the leather bridle, signal of a new start on land, a pipe when he felt the mood at night; no, listen for the poetry that had left him, strangled with the past before he was born, a man of too much feeling and vision spending too much time chasing the fate that would kill him; sleeves out of his shirt, neck goitered and face scarred, arms snake-bitten, his work amounting to nothing, rookeries destroyed by sheep and cattle; he came here returning from that infernal island where he found his woman buried, body without a head in a grave the size of a baby's; came here to die, kill himself by eating of the land, chewing soil and drinking in freezing storms, chains around his neck when the lightning drew close; each afternoon in the days that followed the deaths he gathered up a handful of this dirt, soaked still in the blood of slaughter, and ate it carefully. See how rich it is; and yet we frail mortals cannot absorb it. Streptomycin.

I received the dirt from his hands.

Yes, he continued, not far from here he received his spear wound, a crude pneumothorax, the almost-fatal barb without which he would not have breathed, and when he visited the island, when he found WORÉ dead, decapitated like a wallaby, legs stiff and bent foetus-like when he exhumed the body, he became the killer that he was ... he had come to the moment, you see ... there was no reason, just that coming to the moment ... single-handedly ridding the island of anything that breathed ... marooned sailors, itinerant whalers, escaped felons. He lived on muttonbirds, learned to remove the small gland from the stomach, squeeze out the oil, mix it with honey and swallow it slowly. It cured the cough. But he had seen the settlements, the native enclosures, the institutions. He had seen the kinds of settlers they sent up from Hobart. Someone must have known about it. Someone must have been keeping records. The *idea* must have come first ... and after that always following like the Angel of Death, the gratuitous act.

I've relaxed, he said. I've slept, dropped the oars to look at the shoreline, drifted in and out of lagoons admiring their beauty ... and yes, it was beautiful, but I lost my purpose. I fell in love and almost drowned.

I knew who he was then.

Sperm wasn't writing a novel, Byron Johnson said. He was on a punitive raid.

The waves spat up onto the rock-face, mist curling over the top; clouds scudding low; the grass engorged; muttonbirds weaving a threnody of notes across the sea; it grew dark and I felt a tremor in the soul. I liked masquerades, but not the responsibility of catering to madness. I knew how much like rolling thunder that was ... I knew too, the gentle, disconnected nights of holding a mute sister in my arms.

Ainslie said you were fair.

He took a deep breath.

That too is absorption, he wheezed.

You've got it wrong, I said. We're none of us black anymore.

Yes ... he answered, watching a tern arc its flight across the sky, those familiar grey, angled wings, smoky-cold, like Antarctic ice ... but the intensity serves its purpose.

He pointed.

That bird surpasses itself in the joy of flight. It'll die on some ice floe, without desiring at any time to move to the tropics. But its flight transcribes something for us ... the shape of a thought unthought: its anonymity both its joy and sacrifice.

He turned to me and smiled. It's not alcoholism ... it's not what you think.

I wasn't thinking that, though it crossed my mind ... the jaundiced symptoms, liver malfunction, minimal eating ... these could bring on a deep tan. But he had gone beyond that. His pigmentation cells, the melanocytes, had already started their own revolution, increasing their activity with sunlight; anarchy, perhaps. The degree depended of course, on that mischievous enzyme tyrosinase ... and the injection of copper.

He turned and began walking down the sheep-track.

I would appreciate it, he panted, if you don't mention me to Ainslie. It's not relevant to her.

I was determined, however, to meet with him again, involuntarily learning his mimetic association with the past ... already the nervous tic, already the sardonic smirk passing through him to me.

Not fixed yet, Byron Johnson was thinking as he returned to his room in the hotel. That's what that fellow McGann doesn't seem to realise. We're not fixed in our deadly purpose of grand folly. How therefore to construct the work? Bring about the act itself? Let whosoever dare sign here:

Thomas McGann indeed. His name brings pain to these stern intercostals. No succussations of laughter driving down the gall yet; just the visigoths of the night; pathetic dreaming of gaol cells, and like all dreams, were visitations from the Devil; out, out, dreaded succubi, Oedipal analysts! How you have diminished us! Ah, disinfectant come to save me from their smell! They've cleaned out the vomit from the previous night. Good for them. That's something to count on in a family hotel. See this dreaded limp ... from stumbling many times, for many years ... long attenuated by weights, balls and chains in the best health clubs, preparing, waiting, longing for the next oiling season; oh, how she hung above like an adamantine star in a tempestuous sky, while her patient, impatient, roiled in wetted illness: Emma, dear Emma, no vision nor persuasion from an austere past were you. So there; your cloven-hooved author has sent word ... by appearing, wholly present ... well, maybe not quite whole; aha! A pressurised can of deodorant which will presumably mask the mask of disinfection; there; stinging perfumery far wilder than castor. Heave ho. Reach for the starched beaver. Retch. Again, no. No need for the surgeon's muzzle now. Things are gathering apace; pestilence, plagues. Sweet anaesthesia, how coincident such dreams and acts under your authority! It was imperative a McGann would come to record it all. No, not the vomit. McGann's flickering paleness gives him the authority. For this skin of mine has silenced the inauthentic, endowed a potential simply for action, not words.

Wait. No doubt about that. Draw another syringe from the velvet-lined case. A gift. Hold it like a cigarette. Into the thigh. Extinction. No longer white, unquestioning, biblical. No more dreams of primogeniture and ownership. No longer an author. What a relief. That McGann came running. An amanuensis; a porte-parole; a vicarious vox. There's profit in playing him like a fish, teasing out his sincerity and then to pounce upon his twin. Nothing to lose; a double agent to fate; plan and yet unplan; build and explode.

Why do we seek love upon death, from which others are quick to run? Why, to balance the books of course;

fill the emptiness of the final hours with an illusion we were still capable of a goal at the final whistle. But the result is always a foregone conclusion: love – 0; death – 1. Tired. Enough. The lava's cold, like stone. Here, the form of a human soul. Something there that nags me though, a missing emotion.

See this sodden letter ... sent by the proprietor of the café where I used to work ... Stromboli himself ... to say my mother had ... gone ... passed away in the night ... she'd arisen for something and fell, hit her head on the side of the kitchen table ... that awful laminex from which she was always slipping to the floor ... cut herself open and died that way ... blood strewn all over, so they didn't know at first whether she had been the victim of foul play. Yes, Stromboli always harboured intentions. Of becoming a writer. His description profited from distance, though at the time of reading it passed me like a blur. He had polished it as a kind of elegy, and that made me doubly guilty. So there it was. Claustrophobia at the hands of others. They'll expect me to go back. Not my mother though. Not her. She'll expect me elsewhere. *I'll be along shortly,* I cable Stromboli. *But don't wait up.*

Four o'clock. Walk down three flights of concrete steps. Children playing in the spa, seeming very happy, laughing and giggling and ducking each other, surfacing and making faces. Smile back at the innocents. The afternoon walk past the kitchens and round to the back where they stack the bottles and cans and empty beer kegs. The ground wet, garbage cans crawling with maggots which are making off wriggling toward the grass when I stir them with my boot, the grease-trap clogged and overflowing and the cleaner who likes to be known as a greasologist, though hard to see where the *logos* was involved, says not a word nor has ever been known to, digging out mounds of fatty substance; peculiar smell with a pungency all its own; dogs barking, couple of large German Shepherds tied near the bottle-department which I silence and unhook and let them slurp and jump and wag and we all go for a walk to terrify cats. I'm black and in my element. Though they didn't have dogs to hunt with and were therefore superb hunters, great survivors in a harsh land, wind-chill pulling below zero, wrapped only in wallaby fur, maybe stitched possum vests and bare flesh and head covered in layers of grease, fat, wax ... and understanding which substance had purpose and which ornamental, had several words for grease and so were the true and original greasologists.

Watch the waves swirl into grey slop. Night moving inexorably onward and the erstwhile writer feels these cold pebbles underfoot. This, the substance of the world: counting-stones. Nothing here but the grand folly of infinity. Let me lay them down, one after one, for that is the only way; no metaphysics, no fancy, no belief in the common experience. Rise. Shake off the wet sand. Over there, the end of the beach indistinct in smoky spray and mist, further on past more curvaceous beaches piked by sentinels of submerged and jagged rocks, further round again ... are sharp points, horns of unicorns, white apophyses streaked with lime; over there, the outline of my body, beached in froth like a jellyfish.

There, I had the undifferentiated experience of a critical and voluptuous state, my howls informed by primary and unsocialised rigour. Listen. Hear how detached now, this dry observation. And there I met a woman, and we were joined by a shared circumscription of the letters of passion and fury, before we were both split apart by a different season of the mind ... or by the rituals of gender, I know not which.

She told me what had happened at Cape Grim, and I said to her, I want to go there; to see it.

To see what was happening.

Sperm McGann spurred his horse up on to the rise and saw a cloud of dust. A mob of sheep making for open ground, stumbling, jumping, and in among the grey and white there were natives, running with them. He reined in the horse and felt his heart beating. His condition had made him over-sensitive to sight and sound. He looked to the right and saw in the low scrub men dismounting, saw them kneel and heard musket fire which seemed to have two reports, saw the smoke, heard the slapping sound which brought down sheep, men, those who crawled; saw animals kick over, natives trying to seek cover, women tripping, running one-legged and stiff-limbed, one or two children clinging on. The firing didn't stop. Then the horses came down into their midst and soon the sheep went one way and the Pennemuker people the other, making for the sea like lemmings, irrationally, illogically, leaping, leaping and leaping.

Soon nothing but the sheer cliff and haze of dust; water glistening, waves pelting ashore one or two bodies, arms asunder waving like kelp.

NOWHUMMOE! they had cried, coughing, panting,

feeling the contractions in their chests.

And the waves boomed into the sea-caves.

Sperm McGann saw them tumble from what is now called Victory Hill. Heard the thudding of bodies onto rocks; saw the slow ragged waves beat back the shapes and drag them out and the white men reining in their horses from the edge, some turning and herding back the sheep without waiting and a trio cantering back and forth firing at the waves. Saw the devil.

Nowhummoe.

McGann sat and watched and felt nothing, his horse stepping over spears wedged furtively in the buttongrass, beads of blood clinging crimson and black on the weed stalks, and then he gradually fell into himself, into some secret, indistinguishable pleasure wrapped in grief as he saw the swell lift what was left into the smoky and cavernous ovens of the earth. The slaughter was neatly hidden and buried. They won't return; that was the last of them, he said to himself, his lungs rasping, and he looking to the reddening hills for a distant promise of rest. In the shadows through which he rode he smelled the shale breath of the cold and the wet and rotting vegetation, and jumped the moss-caked logs, feeling the cramp in his thighs.

Not far from the road to Cape Grim. It was night. There was a grassy knoll near the sea. Emma's ute crunched and bounced over the hidden rocks. She led the man who had come from the sea towards the fires spaced out in the caves beneath the cliffs, where the birders would gather to wait for boats in the oiling season; amongst the illuminated shapes of the past; the soft dancing and the lion-maned silhouettes of greased and ringleted hair; the sighs of time squeezing out of burning driftwood, white husks collapsing into the redness; she led him among the errors which would never be righted, amongst the disregard and the neglect and the trammelling of centuries. She stopped on a patch of sand and made him kneel down. And then she removed her tee-shirt and in the flames he saw her ochre-dusted breasts, tattooed, one word above each: *Whitey Sucks*. Mica in her hair like stars.

She had spread pine needles on the sand. He lay back on them and heard his own voice, far back in time, during a Christmas in Hammersmith, and saw his father dressed like Santa Claus pushing a woman in a thin dress up against the wall of the pub.

Then the air was beaten by the blades of a machine and he saw sand sifted through the light, deep rumbling now, the beach shaking. Caught between the devil and the sea, he saw the natives run towards the cliffs. They were swift in the bush, but here moved ungainly, like seals over rocks. Only the women could swim, but the sea was no haven and it began to rain; hot pellets pushing them under.

They are here again, she said.

But he was losing consciousness by then.

Now he watches the dogs gallop over the ridges of sand, sending up bursts of gulls. He squats down near the water and looks out to sea, and then allows the tears to stream down his cheeks and onto Stromboli's letter.

Tom McGann decided not to tell Ainslie her ex-husband had turned up.

The locals talked, sitting on their porches watching the tide come in and out. They talked about Ainslie with her plummy accent, living with a fella who had black blood, a half-caste what's more, who made a helluva racket about land rights and was pushing out fifth generationists, they were saying. Then these women on motorcycles began arriving and staying for weeks at a time. And then there was that black fella with a cockney accent, not an Abo, no, but one of them Jamaicans, Pakis, tourists they get out here when they're not playing cricket or rioting ... fell off a boat dead drunk, they said, and they had to send a helicopter for him ... one of those real black ones ... they were saying when they came into the newsagency to collect their magazines: *Bikes and Boobs, Body-building Babes, Truck 'n Trailer.*

McGann crossed the street in front of the newsagency while the locals watched and when he was just within earshot began to talk more loudly. He walked slowly up the hill. At the brow of the hill he would turn right into Travers Lane and at the end of the lane the dirt road began and went straight out into the countryside and he would follow the creek a little, beating his way along a track parallel to the road, and then cut up through the bush along a fire trail, crossing the peninsula, dipping now and then into rainforest and again into low-lying scrub and heath and some swamp grass spiked with balls of spoor, then forest again, tree ferns so tall they formed a canopy above him, and then presently he would come to a gate, a cattle grid over a small stream. Down the track a little more, and there it was: the wooden house almost completed, skylights in the roof, a deck hoisted on trestles above the canopy of rainforest from which you could see the water, the passage emerald green between the islands, once spouting with black whales. Ainslie's house. Her goal to craft in isolation a structure in the wilderness and in the meantime they ate, slept, lived in an aluminium caravan rocking in the wind like a tiny sailboat in a sea of tea-tree. There's courage there, he was thinking, and had been watching her for months while she and the other women scurried around with beams and lintels, marking out oregon and huon and cypress with chalk at the joins, numbering them, cutting fox-tail wedging and tenon joints and dovetails and housings, checking the mortices and dowels, bracings, struts, studs ... there's courage there too, like a lone bird he saw winging its way across an ice-grey sky, and he felt dispossessed, as if all conviction had been stolen from him. For Johnson, too, had conviction, changing his skin knowing he would never be authentic, but articulating something there as though injected with a divine mission. What were these people doing here, they, who all had a beginning made for them, both materially and psychologically, when he, Tom McGann, staked a patternless existence in his own land where even the government's policy was drift, his stump useless in organising meaning for himself? For after that house fire he had started at the age of four, they were supposed to complete the plastic surgery, extend the bones, but somehow they forgot, his family out of pocket, the agencies neglectful, and so one carpel remained and waggled out of a web of skin ... here, look ... and this rarely enunciated notion of himself was as frangible as the frost which still lay in dark patches underfoot where the sun had not yet entered.

He hears the Volkswagen. Ainslie has returned from town with supplies; nails and more nails. He sees her winding the steering wheel by the handle. She walks towards him angrily, he can tell. She's looking fit and tanned and has muscles in her arms. She doesn't carry any parcels, but throws a book down on the table, making the whole caravan thunder. He knows the book. He's read it from cover to cover, standing in a bookstore in Hobart for an hour without moving. It is Byron Johnson's latest novel. Ainslie opens it, lays it before him. She tears out several pages and holding them in her hand, begins to read bits and pieces:

> You know anything about her politics? A's father was asking.
>
> No.
>
> Me neither. But ever since she was a girl she was always on the radical side, you know.
>
> He waggled the club. Here. Just smack the ball. Imagine a little white bottom. Keep the head down

> and think of a chain hooked from your nose to your balls. A chap wouldn't want to jerk about too much.

Shit, Ainslie says. He didn't even have the decency to mask my name.

Ainslie's face is red. She used to faint when she became emotional, but now she is as cold as a dead bream.

This is supposed honesty, she goes on. Honesty taken to the nth degree. It's bloody manipulation and betrayal. Letters of the alphabet. I hate that. Just like that what's-his-name ... begins with K.

> A's father handed me a small wallet containing five credit cards.
>
> There's a limit on each, he said, but if you're resourceful, you'll find her and have some left over. Bring her back for me.
>
> His eyes were glazed. We were on the green and he fished another club out of his bag.
>
> Now when you're putting, imagine hair around a hole.

Shit, Ainslie says again.

She walks over to the cupboard, takes out a packet of cigarettes, taps one out and lights it. The air is filled with the sweetness of tobacco. She draws on it and coughs.

He's here, she says. I know that tone in his work. I know he's here.

Without saying a word, McGann sweeps the paper off the table, reaches forward, putting his hand into her blouse, feeling the sumptuous weight of her breast. She closes her eyes. Turns her head away. Moans softly.

Yes, she says. You've read it. How am I portrayed?

Go ahead. Put yourself on the line. Know about palpability.

Byron Johnson stuck out his arm and rolled up his sleeve. Touch. Feel.

The sky glared metallic and then the clouds built up and soon a dark tinge crept up the coast.

What's this?

He gave me a plastic tube, crimped at the ends like a bratwurst sausage. I felt the weight of it, sniffed at it. The weather, fast closing, brought on a premature dusk. A fishing trawler rounded the point with a rapid heartbeat and made for the breakwater. He took the tube back from me. Put it into the inside pocket of his coat.

No, sorry. This.

From the same pocket he took out a pen. An old-fashioned dip-pen. Gold-nibbed by the look of it.

My father gave it to me.

German words inscribed on the stem. I gave it back to him. He thought for a while, holding it in his hand.

It would have been simpler for Sperm McGann to lie low, he said, living like other sealers, collecting muttonbird and then blending into the new settlements as a potato farmer or fisherman. It would have been much simpler. Nobody would have noticed.

He shook his head.

The wind is whipping up the waves though the tide is out and the sand is lined with scallops of froth and weed while Sperm McGann looks down the beach watching for the man to emerge from the shack, has seen him once or twice coming out to urinate, throw something from a pot, scrub his feet on some driftwood. Still cold. Now he's taken an axe into the scrub, can hear him felling a dead tree, strokes hollow as a shovel on a skull, and presently a silence, hears the tree creaking and then whumping down and a few minutes later there is the steady bite of a practised blade, and sees the man return with blocks of wood, smoke drifting from the shack. McGann inhales with a hunger for it. Still shivering.

In the late afternoon streamers of sleet had cut lazily through the trees and he'd stumbled along the bank of the creek, trying to make a crude lean-to with broken saplings, and had sat under it watching the skinned trunks glowing white in the strange light, water dripping mercilessly and relentlessly onto him and he'd held himself shivering, cradling the new gun he'd traded for his horse. Just one cartridge he had, wrapped in cardboard and greased with pig-fat, crimped, waiting in the breech. German words printed on it. He took it out and sucked on it and cupped his hands, breathing into them. Then he took out his knife and cut around the base of it and re-inserted it. He stepped into the creek and in a few seconds felt the water soak through his boots and plashed irregularly along, pawing at branches and picking off last season's spiderwebs, and soon found himself looking down the beach, behind the bark shack.

Sticky leaves and bark swirled near the opening to the gravelly beach. The man came out and coughed, softly, like a tiger snake. McGann aimed. Too dark. The man disappeared again. Nervous of showing himself. Had a good sniff that time. Maybe he could smell another human. Couldn't stay there forever. McGann climbs over the bank, crouches down, bellies over from side to side like a lizard, dragging his gun. Gets even closer behind a tussock of grass. From there he would get a good shot off to the back of the head next time. He chews on the leather sling which tastes cold and bitter. Remembers biting into the leather harness as he flailed with the axe at Mrs Bosanquet and the preacher like some mad horse, wrenching himself free from the pathetic defences of the man of God as he tossed, whimpering, a severed hand at him ... remembers the blood-rimmed afternoon and the peace of that river wherein he sank his toes. They had abandoned him, one after the other, beginning with his mother. When the soldiers grabbed him on that bitter Liverpool afternoon, she had dissociated herself. He had been thinking, these latter years, whether he had been her child. Didn't all mothers die for their own children?

He was dizzy from hunger, his head alternately numbed with cold and flushed with fever. He waited awhile and then stood up. Did a kind of callisthenics, whipping his arms about like windmills, twisting his body, bending and touching the sand. He began to jog up and down in place, mesmerised by the sand and pebbles which kept filling the holes where his feet had been. The darkness had crept over the water and somewhere a bird squealed. The light hurt his eyes. He blinked a few times when the door opened, such was the roaring fire within. He crouched, flipped the gun up to his shoulder and squinted along the barrel. He found he was trembling. He brought it down and caught his breath, felt the weight of it in his hand, ran his finger along the fretwork in the butt, tested the hammer again. He brought his left foot forward, rested the gun on his shoulder. He was steady this time, feeling the pleasure of holding himself in this scene, this moment, nothing in the past, when the moment of mortality transforms itself into amnesia. He always used to regain it ... life, the reckoning with the eternal. A moment now, just like the others. A good hero. He was going to be a good hero. He lined up the sight bead with the top of the shack, the white bark providing a good background and when he heard the shuffling, stood up to fire.

Cavalho's head appeared; that familiar round and shaven head. McGann steadied. He scarcely felt what had entered his back then, so great was the shock. A pounding, a seizure in his lungs as he was knocked forwards, the harpoon sending blood into his throat and his heart couldn't rally and he was dead already, his eyes glassing over. Cavalho whistled to his partner. She came from the shack shivering with the blast of cold baying along the cliffs and stared at the body convulsing now, its mouth in mortal rictus, and shook her shaven head to say it was still living. No, Cavalho said. Him's bounty meat now. He went inside and fetched a pot of melted wax and the broad-bladed axe and when he came out again the spasms had ceased and he set to work.

A waxed head appeared in a Royal Easter Show tent in Sydney in the 1950s, accompanied by pieces of firearms, clubs, harpoons and an obscure text about the violence of the early Tasmanians. The wax was sooty and grey.

I go everyday now, to the hotel to meet Byron Johnson. He's got a job as a groundsman and has adapted well, exhuming his working class instincts. He has a room on the ground floor, near the grease trap.

He's taken a liking to me on account of my sister Emma whom he talks about every now and again and then circumvents the topic like a heeler worrying a mob of sheep. I have to keep telling him she's maybe up at Flinders, maybe somewhere else, another island, wherever there's work.

On his rostered day off we usually drink several courses, then we shore it up with half a sandwich or a bag of chips or maybe even a gristly steak, and then we drink some more to wash it down, the fake-blonde woman at the bar refilling the same glasses to save washing, and pretty soon the afternoon is upon us like a bag of wet cement. Then we have several stiff ones in order to linger in the fug of the after-meal, despondent with satiety. After that, a few cleansing ales. The dogs are under our table.

Byron says he's got a credit card to cover all this, though I doubt that.

He's turning blacker.

He says they don't call him Mr Johnson anymore. They don't call him anything. They don't even see him. Worst of all, Cootes the barman wouldn't serve him. Cootes, sitting on the stool behind the bar as though he were a customer, propping his shit-caked boot up on the shelf of washed glasses, once tied his dog up on the bullbar of his Ford Chieftain and then drove off drunk, forgetting the dog was there, later finding a collar and cursing the mongrel for getting itself loose.

Byron is so black he's sick with the toxins in his system, sick from injecting himself with melanotan, sick from the carotene overdose of vitamin A in his liver. He takes out the German dip pen from his pocket and gives it to me.

Take it, he says. It has pierced my side.

It's thin, like a conductor's baton. He says it has made a wound from which he will never heal, that all his life he was moved more by art than life and now he feared most of all the emptiness.

Use it, but don't be confined by it.

He speaks dramatically, as though others were listening. Muffled castanets of ears as the dogs shake.

I did you a favour, he says.

His grin shows a degree of pain.

What favour?

I threw your book in the Thames. The judges never read it.

You call that a favour?

No good you trying to win prizes. Accolades exist for one reason and one reason alone.

What?

To silence you.

That was your favour?

It's the greatest antidote to dishonesty. That other thing …

He struck his heart, hand rough-hewn in eloquent metamorphosis from word to work … and failed to complete the explication of what else was in his pocket.

Your Honour,

He asked if I could bring the Volkswagen next time I came and I said okay and drove every time after that, first to listen to him talk about the garden, native, he said, full of deciduous beech, native laurel, leatherwood and fern, and the birds, honeyeaters, black jays, magpies, cockatoos, and I watched him scurrying about with his *Juncus* reed basket, pruning savagely all the foreign plants they'd put in, helped him mow the lawns and edge the drive, empty the bins and when he knocked off drove him around, usually up to Northmere, along the dirt roads running towards the station and then along the cliffs, passing through several gates which said Private Property, the car bumping over cattle-grids, before heading north to the weather station, circling and then driving back. Sometimes there would be black ducks gliding in on a dam and I'd stop and set a rat trap with bread and sail it out tied on fishing line and it would take no time at all before we had a fire laid down on bark and duck roasting on a griddle, seasoned with herbs B.J. had brought, and we'd have black tea and I felt my childhood crawling up on me, rye grass tickling my neck. Those were good times; the times one never had; the time that was deferred, past and forward, as if the present moment didn't, couldn't possibly exist. It was his birthday. I made a mark in my journal with the stylus.

He was finding it hard to breathe at times, so we drew up at pubs on the way back so he could be sick and then we would have a few drinks and he would be sick all over again, saying black duck didn't agree with him.

I said Ainslie knew he was here.

He nodded, but didn't say anything.

In the afternoon we scoured hardware stores and he was looking for particular things: some rope, oilskins, wire, a knife, electrical pliers. Then I said I had to return with Ainslie's list: coach bolts and planing saws and sanding discs, the night coming on fast and the first icy breaths of moisture sweeping upwards from the ground before it mingled with woodsmoke.

We went our separate ways then, Your Honour. The pleasure's all mine. Don't mention it. This courtroom's like a colosseum. I have experience of these theatres and pray, even less mention of the operation in case the myth doth live, Sirrah. The truth? Here's the pen he gave me. Inebriated? Contempt? If it pleases your lordship. I prefer unreliable. Ask others. Subpenis her. Ainslie Cracklewood. In royal succession.

Ainslie the Absent, you might as well call me. Always the absent. The woman. But I tend to the ordinary things now, no longer eager for theories or the switchblade, determined not to be a literary moll. I've always had good self-esteem.

I rise early, hire day labourers. No man need apply. I saw timber, compute the geometry of roof battens, roll a joist faster than you can say Ainslie Cracklewood. I carry a nail-gun. For the *ongles,* if you'll excuse my Irish. When the morning sun warms the resinous wood something stirs. Creosote fills my nostrils, confuses my tongue, sawdust pecking like pullen at my privates, pollen clinging to fine hairs. Others have been attracted in the past to their blondness. Blow. The sinuses not what they used to be.

Still, two men once adored me, in love with privilege. See how the first time they both — strange this twin incipience, this common novitiate of the working class — they both kissed the soles of my feet, and I, crushing their snaking tongues, told them no, and no meant no. How they adored. I listened to their saccharine implorations as they put me on a pedestal, paying courtly love simply and vulgarly on account of what I represented. Notre Dame. That's what I'm building. A cathedral ceiling. Let no man enter here. See how as I turned away they would have wept, so delicately, each asking if it was all right to kiss me here, or there and finally each at the height of repression, begging for release, when I, already a multitude, an epidermis of tingling pores, a field of disbanded desires, an effulgence of rivers each flowing into an ocean of women, when I simply wiggled and jiggled a few times for them to be spent like poor weeds sown in haste, blown in a slipstream by some dusty country road. How feeble. See how they used to chafe in public, in Stromboli's café, when I rubbed my silken legs and did not have to feign indifference to see them captured in a field between their attraction and my disinterest, and they became swivelling magnets, alternating currents, dynamos which I delayed, deferred, broke down, restarted, prolonged, overheated ... and then performed my own damp and resisting osculation to flower in powder rooms with friends, the door locked, nipple against nipple, mouth to mouth, and then equal and opposite directions without the gross necessity of an extra prodding and inconvenient appendage, finally fulfilled and disturbed in that gentle, wet, deliquescent commingling of scents, in the infinite and eternal waters of the balneum of love; thence to float back out to hot and desperate men, kissing each on the mouth to bring them news of another world, of the familiar and strange, of the decentred, oh, glorious! ... I was the cynosure of neighbouring ayes, the omphalos of the constellation, directing eager sailors to the most delicious and puzzling taboos of the age only to watch them shipwreck in shoals of sperm; yea, yes. Dumbly they pleaded the affirmative case, unable to distinguish the source of their pleasure or displeasure. Thus I gave myself to them with contempt and this was new to them, a woman still evolving, and thus too, I taught debate and not passion, initiated sex with electro-shock, stealing words from dear old B.S., in the end, alas, infected with his prolixity.

Yet there was still a desperate contradiction occupying every waking moment of my life ... the need for separation and the commonality of that need; dissociation and the ass's tail of blind connection; giving the lie to universality or the tongue to puritanism ... until Tasmania. Where I discarded all for intentional misuse.

Discard my overalls now. Take the sun naked on the unfinished verandah. Such simplicity. Stare at the contract labourers through my sunglasses: two women with tumult on their faces. I turn over, imagine their dilatory excitement and control, which is both curious and brave and I make it hard for them with my porcelain accent and my born-to-command tone. They are desperate and polite and maintain the distinction between labour and capital. So I watch the sweat on their arms; young, oh so young; and by dusk they are gone. I reset the beading, nail down the skirting boards, fulfil the contract with a practised hand.

Impossible to find decent help these days.

Byron Johnson is turning even blacker. Blacker than most mainland Aborigines, blacker than any American Black, blacker than most Africans, except for perhaps a degree of blackness found on the Ivory Coast or in the Sudan. He makes people around him peculiar in their pinkness, in their hues of white and brown and freckled amphibiousness. From shades of invisibility he has suddenly become noticeable. It is more a notoriety, for people patronise him as though it were a malady. They open doors for him. They smile inanely without looking at him. Some feel guilty, but they don't know why. Others cross the street so they will not be embarrassed by their own reactions. Still others are just plain contemptuous.

He is now a local identity. They see him driving Tom McGann's Volkswagen around; the one with the soft top and the sign on the bumper which says: __sabled Driver.

He drives out to Northmere on the private road, rippling over cattle-grids. Sometimes he takes the little-used track out to Cape Grim and climbs down to the water, marks the distance to the fresh-air monitoring station with the hip bone of a dead cow buried in kelp, its stomach sunken to a leather bag, a mass of worms and sea-lice emerging from every orifice. He runs his hands through it. A tingling sensation. Putrid smell everywhere. Sometimes he parks on a bush track and sets up his camera with the telescopic lens like an old sea captain searching for spouters. He studies the movements of station hands, waits for the gold Range Rover of Julia Dickenson to emerge and head towards town. He sees sheep raking up a pall of dust along the cliffs and hears the rapid clip of muttonbird wings; smells them as they snap through the air. He follows with his swivelling scope the Range Rover returning to Northmere at nightfall, walks the cliffs lighting great bonfires of leaves and branches, all the time in his ears the shouting and the screaming of the PENNEMUKER; the PENDOWTE; the TOMME-GINNER; the PEE-RAPPER; the MANEGIN.

Some days he drives back past Circular Head, turns off into the hills behind and uses his lens to watch Ainslie Cracklewood, her blond hair tied in a ponytail. Several times he drifts into his narcolepsy, erupts in muffled laughter and falls serenely down into the pale light of a lonely and wondrous condition, the comfort of his mission. At first he muses how all these observations were welded into one plot, but then he realises it was only an illusion, that his office was simply the process of drift, and once he was wedded to it, became an election for life, inaccessible to others. That was the darker path. He descended the hill to a culvert, made his way through the felt of pine needles, stepping carefully over lichens on the deceitful dolerite and crossed the hanging swamp on a rotting boardwalk, corduroyed watercourse of swollen and pulpy logs candied with cottonballs of fungus. Kept his hands in his pockets so he wouldn't grab at the swordgrass if he slipped. Up on the next ridge the shadowline had already risen above the fire trail, sunlight melting over the tops of white-barked gums. His mission and his good sense became intertwined. Sense necessarily sought a clearing, he thought, believing that one truth was ancillary to all and that clarity was a sacred duty having a bearing on the compass of honesty, virtue and character. Well, he had that. Life and death figured in equal parts. He saw it so clearly. He found a small pool, took off his shoes and immersed his feet in it. The water was remarkably warm. He sat and watched insects swim and dart away.

Then he packed up, ate his lunch of pig face leaves, shoots of bracken, grass tree pith and shell-fish, drove all the way back to Stanley and sat in the car behind the petrol station, waiting for the tanker to pull in. Checked his watch.

I encouraged Byron Johnson to fulfil his unfriendly mission. I wouldn't have done it if he hadn't pointed it out first: that death was exactly equal to life.

We had driven that day to Devonport for supplies. He wanted detonators and I took him to Morris McGann's. Morris was my cousin and ran a chandlery in the winter. He sold explosives under licence. When the season was nigh, birders blew channels in the rocks to make landings for their boats. They built up the rubble and made sea-walls, piers, jetties and breakwaters. Every winter these subsided.

Byron and I walked along the mall and people stared. That was how I had always experienced myself, but now I had his skin to prove it. We went into a shop and he bought a yellow Walkman radio. That's when he said that death was exactly equal to life. I asked him what he meant.

See all these people in the street?

There were hardly any. This was Devonport on a Saturday afternoon.

That is life, he said. But that is equally death.

He was fiddling with his radio even before we got out of the shop.

What you are witnessing is an equation that will always be balanced, he continued. One for one. The difference is cosmetic but we invest it with meaning.

He stopped in the middle of the road, seeking some unknown frequency. Luckily there were no cars.

The finality of death is irrevocable ... he swivelled, propped one leg on a light pole ... though the conception of life is fragile and mutable ... yet it is all chance passion and cold death and the middle is nothing but dull perseverance and then it is gone and the equation is completed. It will always be completed.

He looked up at the sky. The question is: which death matters?

And so I encouraged him because I craved that balance. It felt good to be in debt to such equanimity. The emptiness of the streets supported all that. The afternoon glazed over the flat water until the periodic wash of boats sent birds between the derricks, while mulching slime on the rocks swelled and then subsided in deep-green nauseous swirls of hair. *Morris's Shi handlers* stood at the end of a silted dry-dock on a bend of the river, its broken sign truculent with deprecatory humility and uninspired idleness, except for the 'T' some lame-wit had daubed in the space. The afternoon sun, winnowed through loose cloud, glared briefly and faded and then the sky grew dark, long black nimbus rolling in from the sea. Upturned boats unworked for months lay with paint flaking; rope coils eaten by salt and crumbling powdery into grey sand; motors stripped and unrepaired, big props which once churned serious water stranded in verdigris; slip-rails rearing like snakes on a hillock of sand, twisted and perforated with rust; half-buried anchors, shanks just visible as on the seabed; sea slime and weed and lice and crabs seething in yellowing froth; the old hut of raw shiplap listing to one side. For sale. It grew cold.

The receptionist appeared from the toilet surprised, her wedge of a frown transformed from practice into a watermelon smile. She plugged in a tiny radiator. Tested it with a bare foot.

Mr McGann isn't here. Her face said take that or leave it.

Byron sighed. He was threatening to her in his blackness. He wore a beanie which looked like a tea cosy, pinned with badges. He could have been a noble Moor.

Would you like to come back in ten minutes? Friendlier now.

I heard Morris farting from the toilet.

It won't take too long, I said.

That you Tom? Morris was gargling something. Spat a whole lot.

Yeah.

The key's with Carly. Carly, be a good girl and give Tom the key.

I went to the safe. Took out two boxes of detonators. Put a fifty in Carly's hand.

You take care with that stuff, Tom.

You too, Morris. With yours.

Carly bit her lip. Made a face.

Byron had drifted outside. He stood on a jetty watching the *Nora* swing on the tide. I put the boxes into a polystyrene container and wedged it between the floor and the back seat of the Volkswagen. I noticed that he was tracing the edge of the jetty with his foot, testing each board like a tender tooth, saw him pull gently on the rope tethering a painter. Suddenly he was watching me writing, back by the window of the car, his movements invisible. You're never too young to be writing your memoirs, he said.

What do you mean?

Tell me about Emma.

I knew Byron was in love with my sister. I just didn't know how much.

There's nothing much to tell, I said.

Tell me anyway. I get melancholic on cold afternoons. I think about her hair, her face; I imagine a time that could never be ours.

We drove back. I was sure the woman in the back of a taxi we passed was Ainslie, but I was distracted by his discursion on passion ... which he described as a light going out as quickly as a flickering smile, a turn of one's head, and the only marvellous moments as those of transit between the prisons of the heart ... a passionate deferral; a desire never to be released.

It had grown bitterly cold. Curlicues of sleet hung in the clouds.

I don't deserve love then, he said. I know the precise moment at which I failed as a human being.

It's probably not your fault, I said. She's on medication.

Emma McGann knows what's going down but says nothing. She watches everything, notes the seasons, goes birding. She knows he's seen the curious tattoo over her breasts, so she hardly needs to say anything at all to him. She writes poetry which she doesn't need to show anyone ... little scraps of poems which she keeps in her dilly bag along with pebbles which she takes out like tablets when she gets her headaches, counting down the time aloud with them in her mouth for that moment when she will break out of this confusion and into the light. She wears a ring on every finger and dyes her hair. Sometimes it is ginger, sometimes blonde. She walks alone along the cliff tops with her dog and sits in a sheltered cove catching rare summer breezes smelling of warm fur and buttongrass and the fresh clothes on her skin reminding her of a childhood spent swinging on rotary clotheslines staring up at the clouds and the sky with that terrible pain in her chest cutting out a separation ... parents that weren't her own, nothing there that could have been fixed; nothing there that could have existed.

They had a little waterfront place across from Brunie Island, a little fibro house set on concrete piers. At night, in the summers, the possums came down the chimney and ate bread crusts she had left. Nights in bed she'd heard the pop pop of the air gun and in the morning, had seen blood on the carpet and fatty hides hanging in the back shed and the hole which her dog had dug to retrieve the offal. On summer mornings she'd watched the water turn green with the sun and then dark in the afternoons when the storms raged, had imagined whales and whalemen in titanic battle, sailors clinging to the scuppers, the great lash of flukes in the straits. She read and read. In the shed at the back of the yard there were shelves of maritime books and charts. She studied them closely. Knew that she could use that knowledge to chart coincidence.

Then one day he came in, her foster father, lumbering in his shorts and without saying a word, pinned her to the floral settee and lay there for a long time, his sour breath on her neck, silently, heavily, like a whale in his weight, and she was frightened and not frightened at the same time, overcome by the strangeness of it, for it was love and not love and he was tender, but did nothing more until she couldn't breathe and bit him on the shoulder and he winced and drew away and then licked at her bite which was red and wet and she had seen his testicles hanging loose, freed from his undershorts, again overcome by the strangeness of it, the terrible stress and surprise and guilt of knowledge and the curious attraction she had felt to her own power.

The second time they had come from the sea. She had gone up to the north-west to work as a maid on a large station. She was only sixteen, collecting mussels and slivers of rock on a wind-swept cove on her afternoon off, when around the point came a cruiser seeking shelter from heaving seas and she watched it anchor in the bay, saw several men tugging at the chains, watching the big boat sway and drag and then swing into the wind, the motors revving, and saw them fail and return, doing this several times, shouting to each other, quite happy they were, laughing and joshing, slapping one another about, and when the boat finally swung around and held, they congratulated each other, drank and, spying her, waved, soon launching a rubber raft, and motored to the beach, hailed her in a friendly manner, asking her directions and then questions about herself, bringing ashore an esky full of drinks which they proceeded to mix, asking her to taste them and when she said she had to go, suggested she remove her shirt and take the sun while there was some sun to be had grinding hot and glary from the clouds, but she refused and walked away, quite dizzy from the drink and sensing danger walked faster and they had shrugged and said if that was the way she felt, then that was okay; so she trudged off through the scrub and made the mistake of looking back, because one or two then got up and followed her at a distance and when she began to run, slowly at first in that graceful way of hers, and then jerkily and painfully up the hill, she saw they were running too, gaining on her, so that it was like a dream in which she was running in place and they were imploring: Wait! They only wanted to be loved, they hadn't done anything to her, so why was she running and what was her phone number? But she kept running and that fired the primitive in them, a chase, a challenge, hounds and foxes, and they snorted and were bounding after her, naked now they were, stumbling, porpoising from hillock to hillock, great thighs trembling upon her as she was pinned again, playing dead, gasping and shrieking with pain; each again; and she held the heads of those who seemed to care, feeble exploiters of her grief.

Later when she told the mistress of the house she wanted the police, the woman promptly dismissed her, even though the nanny, an English girl called Cracklewood, had interceded.

So now Emma McGann doesn't speak very much. She sees things and says nothing, except that once, in a towering rage at his politics, she had told her brother to go back to the reservation. Things will take their own course. Someone will come along and set the record straight. It's no good remembering, for it brings no comfort. It just creates another hole into which she falls, a temporary amnesia. Why have history otherwise, if not to celebrate the continuity served by ritual, to applaud ritual establishment; the penetration, the amniotic haven of coves and harbours which they prized so much because they came from the sea and needed anchorage in their own reflection, their identity synonymous with conquest? Why have history if not to act, to explode what is necessary? History was a continuity of explosions.

It was then that she began to write letters, feeling such a need to communicate her grief to someone she had read in desperation, who seemed to understand the betrayal of his own mother, of her mother and the betrayal of all mothers beyond her, through the painful dissolution of himself.

What matter who's speaking?

An old man then, who has spent his life charting things.

See her getting out of the taxi, legs first, always those legs, dissolute legs, seems a pity to waste them on other women without at least one male observer. This is a quiet town and we all know what's going on. Here, a butt. Black stockings. Smells fresh. Light. Ah! The principle of the gutter. Shuffle to one side for the gaze to rest on: short black skirt so stocking-tops are visible. Nowadays few stocking-tops, so women looked sheathed all the way to their heads. Nice break in the line. Learned all this working in a manhole. Aha! They never knew what you did down there. The village idiot. Notes from the underground. She dropped a note sliding out of the taxi. Amazing what people drop sliding out of taxis: wallets, cab charges, credit cards, earrings. You could live on it. I did. Like a skunk at midnight; more a bowerbird at breakfast here. Not much nightlife. She walks to a café off the mall. The owner was threatening to close. It was midday. He let her in though, even though nobody else was about, except for a couple of Japanese tourists whom he turned away. Hope they have provisions in their backpacks.

Dear Mr Deakin, the rest torn. Let's see, a smudge of lipstick ... she's unused to this. *My father, Lord Cracklewood* ... something else here, but can't make it out. Obviously a first draft of a letter. Not intimate though. Many first drafts. I've known first drafts. They sting like the wind in my mountain cabin, pages stained with mulled wine, yellowy-red like blood. Now I sit at bus stops watching the automatic teller machines, rushing over after tourists make their withdrawals, see them standing there looking puzzled and then walking away and walking back and then away finally and I dismantle the black box I've glued onto the slot, the notes looking like so many possum skins. *Byron Johnson is a terrorist,* oh me oh my. I think vaguely of London in a winter of bombings, St Paul's crumpling beneath rockets. That was the other war, wasn't it? Got my badge to show for it. A naval veteran. I'm a national treasure and they don't know what to do with me. Demobbed and living in Tasmania, once in a nice house off Brunie Island down south with a wife and an adopted daughter sweet as a new moon, bronzed crescent of a girl, enough! Harmless. My prostate's shot. Trickling here and there like a dog. Relieve myself behind this hoarding. Imagine the slush on dirty London streets, the wet underground thronging with police and harnessed sniffer dogs trailing up and down and taking a leak here and there to confuse the issue. Dogs must be carried on escalators. Purchase tokens here.

An aching emptiness. And yet everything comes out of an aching emptiness.

Stand behind the glass and watch her drink her coffee nervously. There was a black man here a while ago with that no-hoper McGann, who considers himself black but who's really white as a turd from a dying drunk. Black fella spoke with a cockney accent. They all do, nowadays. Sip. That's what upbringing does, little finger rearing from her teacup, no telling what rebellious flag it flies, surely they do it with digits? Don't see how any of that can satisfy, not like men, no, shooting in ecstatic release like a V2. But she is seething beneath. I can always tell when they are on missions of vengeance. A sixth sense. Spurned, perhaps. No longer sought in the eternal quests of men. No longer the stony grail of formidable beauty.

He arrives. Not what she expected, judging by her frown. A man in pin-striped suit and bifocals getting out of a government car. No loose change there. Checks all his pockets.

Just a few beans, mate, for a war veteran.

Piss off.

That's how they treat national treasures these days. I was in the Navy. Knew all about navigation. They never thought to keep me on, use my talents. She rises a little to adjust her skirt. Mr Deakin ... she says, holding out a hand as though it were made of porcelain.

He's watching me while shaking hands, just in case I get near his car ... in case I piss on the tyres like a dog.

I said to Byron on the way back, I said, Byron, do you ever think how the individual is never in command of himself, like the way someone else's voice takes over the story he has to tell and soon there's a chorus and the chorus is like distant cannon fire, the wind melting everything into dust, all the great ideas, and the dust blows into some old farmhouse, sifts a little under a chicken that's roosting on the rafters, a tiny puff ruffling its bum feathers, and all this the end result of a momentous single experience? He thought long and hard and it took a great deal of effort because he had abandoned all this and I could see he was tired of turning experience into thought ... it's the greatness of the world that words are no longer sovereign, he said, truth is simply a language game, and I said no, that wasn't what I meant at all, narrowly missing a kid riding his bike on the wrong side of the road, since kids always ride on the wrong side because they're told to watch the oncoming traffic, watch their oncoming death; no, I said, I mean ... shit. Another one on a bike and this time I've scraped the little bugger's handlebar and I can see he's let loose with gestures and I stick my stump out the window, my extruded finger outdoing the turd in obscenity; no, I said, I mean when you're not in control of who you are, not knowing your place in the world and others begin to tell your story and sooner or later you have no story that's yours. The core is an emptiness.

Byron shifted in his seat. Rejoice, he said. Rejoice that death is inside life.

It took me a while to realise he had his Walkman plugged into his ear and was singing to some scratching rhythm. Another bike coming towards me. This time I really have to get close because a semi-trailer's coming the other way, whole heap of lumber swaying on the curve and chains raining down across the bitumen sending sparks up into the grey air. Hell, I said. Other narratives stem your obsession. A crowd of us without a cause can create havoc; mass death; extinction.

Rejoice! he yelled, that there be no longer signification.

And then it came to me: When I was driving the coach, I said, I used to tell the passengers stories about places, stories I was told to tell; then I started to change them. The passengers got very interested. When we arrived, I would say: look; there's absolutely nothing here. *Nada. Nichts. Niente.* All the rainforests have been cleared. Sooner or later some of the smarter ones would get it. You can always tell. They've stumbled upon loss. Enlightenment comes when you've lost. It would transform their lives. First there would be two, then three, then more. Soon the whole busload would be shaking their heads whenever we arrived at a rainforest or a view. There would be no more life back there, in the place from where they had come. They were now on a mission of liberation. It deferred appreciation; seduced them with death. You see, I said to him, I am like them now.

I was so preoccupied I forgot about the bike and swerved to the side of the road to avoid the flail of chains, narrowly missing the kid, the VW hitting a ditch, bouncing out, doing a rim and the tyre going fup fup fup. I had to stop.

Byron was philosophical. He removed his earphones. It always comes to this, he said; a black hole and some meaning grubbed out of the gutter to impede forward motion.

We ran on the spare to the service station, something clunking underneath, the motor farting and backfiring down every hill, and coaxed the mechanic to hook up the muffler. He donned a mask and began to weld, sparks lighting up the workshop, while I roamed, studying tyres and analysis machines, watching a tanker pull in to fill the underground tanks and thought of the welding and the tanker and the proximity and asked myself how close, what the differential of distance was between the two before the explosion ... when suddenly this fellow walked in, looked as though he'd been sleeping rough, not a good thing to do around these parts, and he stood round near the radiator rubbing his hands together, taking advantage of the fact that the mechanic was under the car and couldn't see him. He was from Germany, Bavaria, he said, and could take this climate, backpacking his way around Tasmania. He had lost some teeth and his hands were blackened, so he seemed to have come from a burnt-out place, his clothes dirty, his boots split.

He told me how the year before he'd been in Philadelphia where the government couldn't run the asylums and the loonies were pushed out into the streets, yes, hundreds of them going on walks round the countryside because they had this pain in their heads, they do that when the pain comes, the talk going on in there telling them they have to keep on the move to where there's no people, trying to get away all the time. Then he was asking me what I thought of house prices around here, how much cars cost, etc., discussing VWs, which he said was the people's car, recalling Hitler had something to do with the design of that because Hitler admired Henry Ford, '*Fordismus*', he called it, which soon became a much respected noun like 'genius'. So someone like Porsche possessed *Fordismus* and designed a people's car, but the war stopped that for a while, progress shifting in a new direction ... and he kept talking as he walked off because he saw the mechanic sliding out from under the car and he had been talking so much I hadn't noticed the welding was over and the tanker had pulled out and when I tried to pay for the welding the mechanic said my friend had already paid, but when I looked around, found that Byron had disappeared, as though he'd departed in the skin of the other man, simply walked off down the road.

I tried the toilet just in case, but the mechanic said he'd gone. Who? Well, he said, I've seen him around before, kind of gone in the head, and he shook his own head saying how the government was shutting down institutions and how they were supposed to be non-violent, but you don't want to take that too literal, he said, wiping his hands with a rag, how would you ever know? They talk a lot, he said, and then he himself spoke no more, turning his attention to another engine.

Fordismus. Maybe Byron Johnson had it, reinventing himself on an unending schizophrenic production line.

I drove up and down the road looking for him but couldn't find him anywhere, so I turned around and drove home. Ainslie wasn't there. For the first time in two days, I broke the seal on a whisky bottle I'd been keeping under my bed in the caravan.

I presumed he took a lift with the tanker driver, your honour ... on my own honour, cross my heart and hope to die; no, maybe not the last. I don't really have aspirations that way. I'm an upright citizen, I pay my taxes when I can.

But you can imagine the kind of desultory conversation, the exchange between working men:

How far you going?

Smithton.

Going as far as Burnie to refill, then to Wynyard. That's as far as I go today.

That'll do.

Looks like sleet.

How often you do this run?

Three, maybe four times a week. Depends.

The less you speak the more you are trusted, Byron must have been thinking. When necessary only say practical things, but only if the information is useful. The motor ran rough. He knew about diesels. Wind gusted in blasts of icy, finger-numbing barrages. The temperature dropped suddenly and then seemed to rise again, gums turning grey when it began to sleet. Burnie's paper mills slung a vast low cloud of white fumes into the hillside. A slurry of bark and sap sucked at the tyres.

But just a moment, your honour. I forgot that Byron Johnson was black.

Start again.

You mind if I grab a lift off you far as Smithton?

Sorry. No can do. Company policy.

Listen. Just get in and drive. See this here stick of jelly? It's sweating. See this detonator? I'll just ease it up its arse and put the whole thing down your shirt. This little wire here? It's electronically tuned to my Walkman, this little yellow-back radio. Very sensitive. Now, let's fuckin get outta here.

Careful with that thing matey, Christ.

And so on. Interminable silences. Necessary trust. The driver's nervous as hell, almost stalling three or four times.

Something's wrong with the motor, he says.

Nothing's wrong with it, Byron says. He knows about diesels.

They stopped at Burnie and because it was raining now, quite steadily, and the air was heavy and dark, nobody noticed Byron in an oilskin and Akubra, filling the tanker at the depot. The driver signed the sheet and they were on their way.

Yet it could not have happened that way either, I beg you all to realise, for the lack of words, the silences, would have prevented the continuity of forward progress, Byron Johnson would have been thinking as he sat in the cab of the semi, for that was the way he used to think, aloud, and not a lot of it made sense, as he sat thinking how he'd paid the driver for a lift at the service station and then discovered a seam of narrative, when in drizzling Burnie the driver filled the tanker and Byron Johnson drove off while the driver went for a leak, heading for Cape Grim, a narrative in his head which would have now become for him a maternal mission, a ritual of obsession, historical continuance, a beacon, an observatory, a monitoring station of fair play. A final equation. It had a wonderful purity.

All this time I sat drinking in Ainslie's new wooden house, sniffing at oregon, cypress, ironbark, the weather closing in outside and he, discovering all the controls in the tanker, breathing in the diesel, working the wipers as he bounced over the dirt roads out on the track towards Northmere. He understood the possibility of undoing the cocks and then driving up onto the grassy cliff tops, understood the rate at which refined petroleum could be pumped out, a mere two hundred barrels while driving around, nobody noticing because once a week a similar tanker manoeuvred to supply dieseline to the station. Standing on the cliff top he could see that petrol had started to fill the caves below and then fifteen minutes later he judged it to be enough for him to flick on his lighter and run a trail of flame over Suicide Cove, cascading over the edge and exploding the caves below.

They lit up like an abandoned and fired hive, incandescence honeycombing the cliff base, cells glowing red to illuminate his second project as his soul descended into the wan light of the dead, wishing McGann was with him, daring him to stay with him, ride with his words, challenging him: Are you too white to do this? Are you free if you don't use your freedom to act?

Then he would drive back and fire the grasses at Northmere as they did centuries or a millennium ago, the wind from South America distilled by oceans, the wind pure and fierce and driven, taking the flames inexorably towards the station. Soon the spires of the cathedral of silence and deception would be glowing, in its heart an empty cave. Oh, a conflagration never to be forgotten, the nave taking the first impact of the runaway tanker, then the choir and finally the tombs disgorging their bishops and nobles, spewing mummified bodies onto the pavement before the altar. *Putains!* he screams, his mind thick with smoke; *putains!* he spits. He was through with bloodlines, lineage, heritage, motherlands, cathedrals. He paused, adjusted the wires and made the connection between the ignition switch and the detonator, feeling the weight of gelignite in his hand, nitroglycerine mixed with wood pulp ... He could see it already: the reconstruction of Nature and the return of wildflowers and muttonbirds, the sigh of the sea.

One by one, page by page, I throw what I have written into the fire.

I would have to take the trip myself. But sodden, sitting naked before the fire in this wooden house, beneath this cathedral ceiling, this atrium or turret which is so imposing over the living room, I lack the vitality, the courage, the will ... all of which becomes reason, and reasonably, I grow old on this night while he, soaked in rain, struggled with the brakes on the truck as it had rolled not more than fifty feet in the direction of Northmere. He found the DD3 actuator, the button which held the mechanical brake, but it was off. So was the hand valve. He had lost the names for things and saw only a black tree against a cold sky; heard the sound of water. Already shouts were cracking the air. He tried to push. Thought of his weight-lifting, the Valsalva Manoeuvre, *an increase in intrapulmonic pressure by forcible exhalation against the closed glottis.* All Byron Johnson knew though, was that there was a pressure high in his chest, and at that moment I couldn't breathe, thinking of WORÉ giving herself to Sperm McGann as part of the negotiation for peace, and I let a burning page waft upwards towards the ceiling. Johnson did not know if he existed either. After all, no one could see him, as though their gazes fell away at the appearance of an extinct species, for they did not know how to look. But suddenly the other pages in my hand catch as well and I try to slap them out and my arm is burned. I sit there waiting for the delayed and terrible pain which I know will come, tingling, searing, and I remember burning paper once as a child and holding my hand over it, an experiment in self-loathing.

There must have been a child.

There was always a child transfixed by burning paper, and now on a windshift, sparks pepper the dark like fireflies, the horizon alight, a thin, luminous ribbon. Yes, on a windshift Byron Johnson saw in the other light streaming from an open French window the unmistakable figure of Julia Dickenson in a translucent nightgown, or a cage of whalebone, saw her turn fleetingly to go back inside, her swollen silhouette framed in the doorway, saw the transformation from imperial glory to the pathetic irony of heritage, shackled to lone assumptions beating into the night, foundering as luffing men o' war seeking purchase on slimy rock; saw love crumbling like chalky cliffs; saw all those ladies with fine naval fervour and mean usage in heated drawing rooms spreading purification and perfume and the Great Tradition unaware of their illegitimacy, bastardry ground away like polenta beneath the deadly rolling-pin of history which continues to build castles from ruins, imperial cathedrals, confident that obsession will not turn like a rabid dog. He knew now what the girl had meant at Ypres, knew that history wasn't everything. He sought the talk-back channel on his radio.

There must have been a child, but after love there will always be silence. His child.

He saw on a windshift how his arson had swept back towards the sea and spared Northmere, saw how Julia had paused ... perhaps longing for the cataclysm, yet another, to take her out of this sheltered nullity, longing perhaps to submerge the cathedral of continuity beneath the sea, to drown forever the spirits within it which haunted her night after night with eerie cries ... when the wind turned the flames harmlessly away, the fire subverting itself, burning itself out, so it became nothing but an upstart idea, a brief and flashing bulb.

Byron Johnson stood on the rise silhouetted in the purple light. He wanted to unburden himself of the weight on his chest; took off his coat, tore at his shirt.

It was the moment when I knew I had failed him, my passion gone; pushed madness over while hungering for ethical reappraisal and historical outrage, unwilling to bring extinction upon my head. It was also the moment when I understood him perfectly. The future belonged not to the imagination but to biology. Simple cells. There must have been a son which Cavalho raised in his hut. There must have been a squalling and a caterwauling, a mewling baby with powerful lungs, breath held only to hear Cavalho's wheezings, the final pulmonary spasms against which it laid its head, to hear the final expiratory curse at the government nurse who duly recorded the name ... McGann ... and who promptly despatched the baby to an orphanage.

And so the wind changed and turned the fire upon that which begot it.

There was a muffled explosion.

It was on the news the next morning.

There were no bodies to be found at Cape Grim. The reports carried a particular refrain, echoed down through the ages, resonant of the fate of so many Tasman explorers, convicts, escapees, dreamers, natives ... there were no bodies, no sir. Vanished into that gaping maw of wilderness or sea, the thick carpet of jungle or water. The incident was seen as coincidental at first: rumours of St Elmo's Fire, a chance lightning strike, a random spark from an electric fence which blew the fuel drums. They did not find the remains of the tanker until later. Even much later, evidence of gelignite. Then it became clearer. The purified wind had changed in a moment of magic and the ghosts had come alive, had begun their ancient practice: the fire always turned in a semi-circle, sweeping back the game; look there, ten thousand breaths speeding cloudy galleons across a clear sky, back to the horizon whence they had come.

Tom McGann packed his things. He had taken heed of too many signs throughout this life and needed to make a path all his own, satisfying the nomadic turn in him which leant far over and sought nothing on the nether shore. He tidied up the caravan, took Ainslie's things into the house, stepping lightly over the charred wood and creeping water, heard the crackle in the early light and listened for a moment to a car to establish its continuing rhythm. He collapsed the roof of the caravan, hitched it to the VW. He took a plastic case from the glovebox, examined the syringes inside ... the vials of Melanotan ... and closed the lid.

He started the car, heard the caravan crunch after him, and drove away.

F*rom the logbook of the* 'Nora' *under the command of Captain Orville Pennington-James. 19th July 1829:*

Fair winds for the first part of the morning. I have a feeling this log will end almost before it has begun. Imagine. Six months at sea and I've written that first line, with slight variations, almost a hundred and fifty times ... to keep the owners happy. They want to read happy stories. Yet today, there is an unusually vinous pungency about this wind whose only previous landfall has been South America and which will touch the tip of Cape Grim some time this evening, wafting a sigh of unusual solace before those elemental cliffs, drawing out the natives towards the sea to view us arriving before it. First contacts are always sentimental ... before the violence.

Thus I, who have never known love, know only of its absence. Its romanticism plays like froth upon the waves and I would presume native cultures have no use for it. Still, I dream of the experience, and deal out the rum. Experience the imagined, willing the capacity to see down one day when a reader of this log will sail these waters, carry off his love and make a fatal turn into history and thus remedy everything I have despoiled by allowing my indignity to remain silent.

Be still, old stomach! I don't need your growling to remind me of hunger and fear. The crew are restless. Tonight, or perhaps the next, they will attempt mutiny. Standing here at the stern, my hand on the wheel, I allow my heart to spark and fail in this most difficult emptiness in the world, uncertain of what it seeks upon these latitudes hereafter: fire or ice.

And now I return to these windswept cliffs several months later.

The muttonbirds have redoubled, mining and burrowing into the soft ash beneath new grass. Emma, if she were here, would have walked down to the sea, wrapping her cardigan around her thin shoulders; would have stooped to pick up pebbles, the wind promising her that the next time what came from the sea would be the answer to the deep longing in her heart, longing for a sail to appear from her words, a longing I knew was not pain, but part of a concentration on small things, like the birds, the wind, life and love.

I remember the soft plateau and the sheep tracks, the dung and the muttonbird burrows, the tussocky slope leading without warning to the precipitous cliffs and the sheer drop into the sea. I remember the Bass Strait winds blowing so fiercely you hung on for dear life to the long grass and prayed the sea wouldn't heave and swallow you up, when you grew dizzy lying on your back holding down your dress, watching the albatross glide in place, wings perfectly shaped to scoop up the wind which was scooping up your dress ... yes, how I remember that!

Gravity had drawn me back towards you. The gravity in you, the gravity of you, which will draw us together, down, deep down, forever.

And thus he had written, in reply to her letters, long before he had met her; long before he had been to Tasmania where love had left him undefended, that lone island within himself dissolving into drizzle, into the salt-spray of soft shapes, into the rich loam of a future coalescence in his watery crossing of the universe.

My sister disappeared on 13 November 1993 off West Point, northwestern Tasmania. They found her handbag filled with smooth pebbles. Counting stones. She was always collecting them; a miscellany of hieratic and positive things. A part of myself went missing as well, and for months after, I had cause to say: *Emma, c'est moi,* and heard nothing of what people said.

What they said was that the first person he called on was her. He had reached her cabin by walking along the cliffs and then swimming across small bays and inlets. The police were already searching for him, a helicopter whipping at the low scrub with powerful searchlights, worrying the coast like an angry wasp. His clothes were charred and soaked, his forearm burnt, revealing a layer of white skin beneath. Emma was not surprised to see him. She rubbed ointment into his arm and wrapped it in gauze. She fed him and lay with him until dawn, and when they emerged in the morning, an armada of small boats had gathered, a flotilla of birders waiting to cross the straits had assembled for him and they were waving and smiling, readying to forge his escape. With unspoken tenderness they lifted him aboard and sped him towards Stanley. Once at the breakwater, they transferred him onto the *Nora,* Morris already at the helm, the diesel motor thumping reassuringly, fanning blue exhaust over the calm water. Three miles out, Morris launched the lifeboat and returned to shore.

These are of course conjectures, and nowadays, probably myths. Some say they saw the *Nora* dipping over the horizon towards the South Seas and its paradisiacal islands. Others say the wind shifted again and again, and that the old barque took a fatal turning in Banks Strait and sailed due south, heading for ice, not improbably, since B.S. Johnson had left a note together with his credit cards, a birth certificate from Hammersmith (which I will use in due course) and his passport, which I've managed to coax from Ainslie. The scrap of paper was the usual writer's memo:

> *A list of ices:*
> growlers
> ice bastions
> ice haycocks
> ice floes
> ice rinds
> ice hummocks
> ice flowers
> ice pipes
> ice wedges
> pancake ice
> frazil ice

vuggy ice
anchor ice
rime ice
ice dust
plate ice
bullet ice
drift ice

Out of habit, a plan to use this vocabulary ... the listing establishing the moment of arrival at a counterfeit reality which he would then discard.

Whatever the case, it is incumbent upon me to put things in order, to relieve the myth of its importance. And so I am going to Hammersmith to set the record straight, to defend him against accusations of insularity or puritanism or of being a minor participant in the great adventure of the novel. I am doing it not because I believe there will be a true reason for his death, nor because I see it as a deliverance from what I cannot understand, but because I feel a responsibility for the asking of the question. *What aileth thee?* It would have been enough for him to let the cup pass, renew himself, redeem himself from that horrendous quest for absolute integrity.

Yes, I shall have to recuperate for B.S. Johnson the startling, dazzling and blinding originality hidden in his suicide (I'm not sure that's what it was; he may have simply been called away and had the capacity to stay under for a long time, take on a new skin), a death that has become mine, forcing me to retrace my steps, working back to tell the story before this one, and in that I am finally, I believe, extremely blessed that he had opened a way. By imagining us, he lit a fire in which he perished. In dying, he pushed the truth beyond its own limit, turning the challenge of supreme honesty upon itself:

> ... what I am really doing is challenging the reader to prove his own existence as palpably as I am proving mine by the act of writing.

The equation is balanced. It made it impossible to live.

On the plane a child beside me has lent me his mystic writing pad ... one of those wax tablets upon which everything written can be erased by lifting the plastic sheet. It must have been the same for Sperm McGann, moulding wax over the dead and lifting it off. It was neither death nor life he was creating. Perhaps it revealed the painful secret of existence: that invention was always the result of repression, censorship and violation. *Nihil ab origine.* Yet, what could be more exemplary than the perfection of one's own death ... in the service of our deepest secret? Byron Johnson had invited me to gaze upon it. Here, I even look a little like him ... all except for this withered arm with its burnt and peeling onion skin and this perverse finger, which I hold up to the plane's porthole as we climb high over Cape Grim ... an involuntary gesture, sign of my eagerness to tell ... (the sheep and cattle down there destroyed, brucellosis on the rampage ... yes, I understand disease ... the child is already taking notes) ... my eagerness to pass on, if you get my drift, to what matters.

To what has always mattered.

Acknowledgments

B.S. Johnson, *Aren't You Rather Young to be Writing Your Memoirs?* Hutchinson of London, 1973.

Claude Lévi-Strauss, *The View From Afar,* Trans. Joachim Neugroschel and Phoebe Hoss, Basic Books, N.Y. 1985, Myth and Forgetfulness.

N.J.B. Plomley (ed.), *Friendly Mission: The Tasmanian Journals and Papers of George Augustus Robinson 1829-1834,* Tasmanian Historical Research Association, Hobart 1966.

Cassandra Pybus, *Community of Thieves,* William Heinemann Australia, Melbourne 1991.

Heather Felton and Geoff Lennox.